RACING STORM MOUNTAIN

RACING STORM MOUNTAIN

TRENT REEDY

NORTON YOUNG READERS
An Imprint of W. W. Norton & Company
Independent Publishers Since 1923

Printed in the United States
First Edition

For information about special discounts for bulk purchases, please contact
W. W. Norton Special Sales at specialsales@wwnorton.com or 800-233-4830

Manufacturing by Lakeside Book Company
Production manager: Beth Steidle

ISBN 978-1-324-01139-2

W. W. Norton & Company, Inc., 500 Fifth Avenue, New York, N.Y. 10110
www.wwnorton.com

W. W. Norton & Company Ltd., 15 Carlisle Street, London W1D 3BS

0 9 8 7 6 5 4 3 2 1

This book is dedicated to Ammi-Joan Paquette,
my wonderful literary agent and dear friend. Ten books, Joan!
Working with you has been one of the greatest joys of my life.
Here's to the next decade and many more books.

CHAPTER 1

KELTON FIELDING SHIVERED IN THE BITING COLD, HIS worn sneakers pushing through the two inches of last night's new snow on the sidewalk. He tried to warm his hands by holding the breakfast burrito in his pocket. Two blocks from home, he stopped and muttered a curse. "Come on, man." The crusty old dude who lived on that corner in an ancient, rusted Airstream camper never shoveled his sidewalks. It had snowed a little every day since the opening of McCall's Winter Carnival last Friday, a great gift for the carnival, but not for Kelton. He would either have to go half a block back down the sidewalk to a cleared driveway and then walk in the street or walk through the thick snow here, trying to step in his partially filled footprints from yesterday, snow falling down into his sneakers, leaving his feet cold and wet all morning.

OK, maybe it wasn't really that much of a hassle to go all the way around, but thing was, the guy kept this scrawny dog chained to a tree on a dirt patch in the backyard. Now the dog made a dirty snow circle with his chain, running around, constantly barking. At least until Kelton approached the rickety wooden fence plastered with ugly orange NO TRESPASSSING signs. As soon as the dog saw him, he quieted down and rushed as close to Kelton as his chain would allow, deep into the weed patch about six inches from the fence.

"Hey, Scruffy," Kelton said quietly. One time the old man had burst out of his trailer, threatening to call the cops on Kelton for trespassing. Kelton glanced around to make sure nobody was watching him. Last thing he wanted was to get in trouble or be made fun of for hanging around a place like this.

He reached through a gap in the fence to pet the dog. "How you hanging in there?"

Scruffy wagged his matted tail and sniffed Kelton's fingers. Kelton laughed. "Wha'? You hungry again?"

Scruffy whined a little. Kelton scratched behind the dog's ears. There weren't a lot of human footprints behind the trailer. When did the old man ever feed this dog?

Kelton pulled the burrito from his pocket, his mouth watering just looking at the thing. Mom had splurged on the good brand, the larger ones that would keep him full through most of the morning. He tore off a big steaming chunk from one end, careful not to drop any egg or ham. "OK, here you go, buddy."

The first time Kelton had fed Scruffy like this, he'd been worried the dog would bite his fingers off to get the food, but Scruffy was careful. He was a real nice dog. In a second, the dog had eaten his chunk and was licking Kelton's fingers. "You're always hungry, aren't you?" Kelton's stomach growled as he took the first bite of his breakfast. Scruffy tilted his head, staring at the food. "Yeah, I know the feeling."

He was sure that, once again, he'd know that hollow emptiness later that morning as he waited for lunch. He handed the burrito to the desperate dog, who devoured it in seconds. Kelton petted Scruffy more, feeling his ribs. "We're finally living in a place that allows pets, but I can't be sure we're staying. Otherwise, I'd take you with me. Just steal you. I don't care."

Kelton had thought about taking Scruffy home lots of times. Just grab the bolt cutters from the garage, hide them under his coat until he reached the fence, lean down, snip the little chain, and carry that dog home where he could be happy. It would be stealing. Fine. But the old man didn't pet that dog or nothing. Scruffy was stuck out there all alone all the time. And it wasn't right.

Snow had melted into Kelton's shoes again. "See ya, Scruffy. I gotta go to school now." Kelton shivered, and Scruffy shook himself, rattling his chain. "Hang in there, buddy." Kelton rubbed his itchy eyes and continued toward school.

Inside, Kelton did his best to scrape the snow from his sneakers on the big doormat. His old worn-out wet shoes squeaked on the shiny school floors, but even with his lightly squeaking footsteps, nobody paid attention to him that morning. Same as a lot of mornings.

He tried to nod at Seth Remmings and Milo Tanner, a couple of guys from the band and science fiction crowd that always hung out in the commons even after the bell rang to allow people to go down the hall to their lockers. Sometimes those two were pretty cool. But today they were too wrapped up talking to each other about a figure-based tabletop game they were always playing. At first it had looked fun, but each of the little plastic medieval warrior figures cost about fifteen bucks, and that was new out of the box. Rare figures on the collector market could sell for as high as $50 or $100. Forget it. He didn't even want to play the stupid game. For real.

"Hey!" Morgan Vaughn squeaked as she rushed up to Swann Siddiq. Morgan flipped her hand back through her sandy blond hair. "What do you think?"

Swann flashed her bright smile, the same smile that had lit up the cover of *People* magazine only last year. At first nobody had believed the rumor, but then someone had found the cover image online and printed the happy family picture of Swann with her famous-actor parents.

"It looks great," Swann said.

It wasn't that great, Kelton knew. He'd never say so around anyone, but he knew way more about women's hairstyles than most guys, on account of his mother working at the Color & Cut Cowgirl salon. Ever since Swann Siddiq's family had moved to McCall from Hollywood, at least four girls—five, counting Morgan—had shown up asking for this special swept look. The problem, Mom had tried to explain, was that certain hair-care products and special curling irons or something were very expensive. To do the style right, a girl would have to pay hundreds of dollars to a stylist who had the right products and really knew the technique.

"Did you get it done at Color & Cut Cowgirl?" Swann asked.

Morgan and Swann kept talking in that super-excited way girls had, and neither of them noticed McKenzie Crenner messing with her books at her locker while she pretended she hadn't seen her best friend and number one disciple cozying up to Swann.

Kelton watched it all. He often noticed things about other people, never being noticed himself.

McKenzie Crenner had always been the most popular girl in the sixth grade. She was beautiful, wore all the newest clothes with the labels everybody cared about so much, and she was super good at volleyball and basketball. When McKenzie thought something was neat or important, so did most of the rest of the girls. Then a lot of the guys would act like they cared too, because they wanted to impress the girls.

When Swann arrived, she blew up the whole system. Her famous parents had recently purchased a $3 million mansion they called a log cabin right on the lake. They'd had a housewarming party not long after they moved in. Kelton hadn't been invited, of course. It was for the Populars only. But nothing had been the same after that party. McKenzie Crenner acted like she thought Swann was great and all the Populars were close friends, but Kelton knew that was a load of crap. He didn't get the best grades, but he wasn't dumb enough to fail to notice the trouble behind those beautiful smiles and fake hugs.

It wasn't assigned seating in science, so Kelton always grabbed a stool at one of the two-person black lab-table desk things in the back. He was less likely to get made fun of back there, and if he was, at least he'd see it coming.

From his backpack, he produced his three-ring binder that his mom had from when she was a manager at the local Gas & Sip a few years ago. He'd cut out the cover insert picture so that it was plain and black. Not the coolest binder, but people didn't make a big deal about the dumb Gas & Sip corporate logo anymore. Packed inside, taking up all the room on the metal rings, were the key sections of the 1,308-page service manual for his 2006 Ski-Doo Summit 800 snowmobile, just the pages he needed to help him finally get the machine running. His mom's ex-boyfriend Darren had purchased the manual online and downloaded it on his work laptop, printing it at home back when the printer worked.

When Darren was still living with them, before he and Mom broke up, the guy used to take Kelton zipping across the white, both on trail and off. Kelton had laughed the whole time Darren had cranked it up full throttle on an easy downhill run. Nobody believed Kelton when he talked about it, but he and Darren had been up to a hundred miles per hour. Off a little snow bump, and they'd had that 445-pound beast in the air. It was old, but that sled used to be able to really move. It would again.

Of course, for a long time Kelton had been too afraid to even touch Darren's snowmobile. He'd never been allowed to mess with it when Darren wasn't around. But now Darren was never around, and Mom had made it clear he was never coming back. "Whatever junk he left behind is up to us to dispose of now," she'd said. That's when Kelton figured the Ski-Doo might as well be his own.

Laughter echoed from the hallway, and a moment later Hunter Higgins, Hunter's cousin Yumi, and Annette Willard entered the room.

Barrett Wilson flopped onto a stool next to Hunter. "How many wolves did you shoot today?"

Kelton sighed. Barrett asked Hunter that every single day. Just because Hunter took a lucky shot a few months ago and brought down a wolf, people acted like he was so great.

Hunter chuckled. "Dad says the wolf should be back from the taxidermist in about a week."

"Cool," said Barrett. "I gotta see that."

"Great match last night, Barrett," said McKenzie Crenner from the front of the room. "A pin in the first period. So cool."

"Yeah, I'd never been to a wrestling game before," Swann cut in. McKenzie's smile turned just a little stale. Swann pushed back a strand of her midnight-black hair. Kelton tried to focus on his snowmobile schematics, but Swann Siddiq did have pretty hair. For real. Swann continued, "My old school only had tennis, golf, track, and gymnastics. It was more arts-focused. But you looked super-tough, Barrett."

Swann was beautiful. But she was rich, and came from Hollywood and an expensive rich-kid private school, and she rarely went through a day without reminding people of that fact.

"Thanks," Barrett replied. Kelton raised an eyebrow. A couple of years ago, he had tried to congratulate Barrett on a good job in a wrestling "game." The guy had done his half-laugh, half-grunt thing and corrected him. That's how he learned that wrestlers did not like to call their sports contests games.

"It's called a wrestling meet, silly." McKenzie laughed. "Not a wrestling game."

"Whatever. Barrett still did great," Swann said. Then she added, to Tannin Gravin, "So did you." The two wrestlers in the class thanked her. McKenzie couldn't even fake a smile after Swann had once again seized the attention.

Milo Tanner sat down on the other stool at Kelton's table, hiding behind his curtain of long dark curly hair as usual.

"Hey, Milo," Kelton said, surprised the guy had joined him before he realized the seat next to him was the second-to-last available, the other being next to one of the Populars. If it were up to Milo, he would have grabbed a stool next to his buddy Seth.

"Hi," Milo said quietly. He said everything quietly. "Get your snowmobile going yet?"

With time running out the way it was, Milo's question somehow drew even more nervous energy from deep in Kelton, like twisting a wet rag draws out water. "Not yet. Still waiting for the part to come in. Everything's ready. Got it started. Got the nine million strings from the old shredded belt finally cleaned out of the primary and secondary clutches." Oh, Kelton hoped that belt would arrive today. If it showed up tomorrow, he might be able to get it installed and hurry down in time for the start of the Winter Carnival Snowmobile Fun Race, although he wouldn't have time to run the sled at slower speeds to seat the new belt, to work it in before he had to go full-throttle in the race. Kelton had spent countless hours after school at the public library, watching YouTube videos about snowmobiles. The mechanics and pro snowmobile guys all said topping the sled out right after a belt change would really shorten the life of the belt.

"Basically, if that new belt shows up today, I should be set," Kelton said.

"That's cool," said Milo.

Kelton was pretty sure Milo didn't know the difference between the primary clutch and the skis, but he at least pretended to be interested. Milo was a good guy like that.

"Still trying to get that old Ski-Doo running, Fielding?" Bryden Simmons said as he entered the room.

"I got it running," Kelton said sharply. Just because Simmons's dad owned McCall Max Motorsports and had simply handed him a brand-new Polaris 850 Switchback Assault didn't mean the guy was master of the snow. "Just need a new belt and it's ready to go."

"Oh great," Bryden said. "So you can start the engine. Just can't actually make the snowmobile move. Awesome." He walked on by as though Kelton had ceased to exist. "Hunter, I know you have real sleds. You racing tomorrow?"

"Not really my snowmobiles," Hunter said. "But yeah. I'll

be racing. Don't think I'll have much of a chance of winning, especially against your new sled, but I'll give it a try."

Kelton snorted a little. The guy's family had a huge hunting lodge on a private hunting preserve, where they kept a whole fleet of snowmobiles, four-wheelers, and everything else. He acted so humble with his "I don't have much of a chance" and "I'll give it a try," but the truth was his family had great sleds and his rich lawyer daddy had paid the race entry for him.

"You racing, Yumi?" Bryden asked.

"I'm not so big on the winter sports," Yumi said. "Some skiing once in a while. No race for me."

"How about you, Swann?" Morgan Vaughn asked. "Your dad is donating that awesome snowmobile, after all."

"A custom Yamaha Sidewinder SRX LE," Bryden said with amazement in his voice. He was right to be impressed. It was the fastest production snowmobile in the world, an $18,000 machine. Some of the guys online talked about driving theirs at speeds around 120 miles per hour. With the modifications done for Swann's daddy's action movie *Snowtastrophe III*, it was said to push speeds up near 150, plus it had been fitted out with cool lights that made it seem to hover over the snow.

"Father won't buy me a snowmobile," Swann explained.

Kelton was truly shocked. Her dad's films had made a ton of money, and the guy could easily swing a few thousand bucks for a snowmobile, not like Kelton, who was in big trouble if he didn't win the race and Mom's boyfriend Steve found out how he'd raised the money for the race entry fee and for the new belt for his Ski-Doo.

"Is it really the one he rode in the movie?" Bryden asked Swann.

Swann's smile faded a bit. "That's what they say." She waved away his question, as if she were done talking about it.

"An awesome snowmobile and half-a-grand prize money?" Bryden rubbed his hands together. "It's mine! I'm winning this thing."

Kelton turned to the last two pages in his binder for proof that Bryden was wrong. He wouldn't win tomorrow's race, Kelton would. At the library, he'd printed a complete copy of the official race rules. The course consisted of a trail seventy miles long, looping around the base of Mount McCall, or Storm Mountain, as some people called it. Thing was, Kelton had read all the rules at least ten times. Racers were required to clock in at each of four checkpoints. Except the rules listed no requirement for racers staying on the trail. From the back pocket of his binder he pulled and unfolded a topographical map of McCall and the surrounding area. Something useful that Mom's new boyfriend Steve had brought when he moved in this last summer, it was the kind of map with contour lines to mark elevation, like the Army uses. Steve had a big thing about how he had always wanted to join the Army, would have enlisted and become a Special Forces sniper except for this legal violation that wasn't his fault.

Kelton printed out an online course map and compared it to

his own. Checkpoints one and two were pretty far apart. Racers would reach the first flags on the straight path about halfway from the starting line to the first curve that led around to the north side of the mountain. The second checkpoint was a few miles down the more or less straight path on the north side.

On his map, Kelton had drawn his path to victory. Mount McCall wasn't much of a mountain, and it consisted of two peaks, Big McCall to the west and Little McCall to the east, with a high valley between them. There was a defunct gold mine somewhere up there, with the rough remains of the old road over the mountain. After hitting the first checkpoint, instead of going way around the mountain, Kelton would cut many miles off his race by going through the pass over the mountain directly to checkpoint two. It had taken the better part of a day to measure the distance on the map against the likely speed of the fastest sleds to figure out he'd hit checkpoint two before the rest of the chumps were even halfway between the first and second.

Kelton smiled as he looked over the map and reviewed his route again. It was a great plan, completely allowable by the rules, and the perfect way to compensate for all the advantages the Populars had with their rich parents and more expensive and powerful snowmobiles. When Kelton won the custom-mod Yamaha Sidewinder SRX LE, he'd sell it, and with that and the $500 prize have more than enough to avoid any trouble with Steve. He took a deep, satisfied breath. For once, things would work out for him.

The bell rang, and Mrs. Wittinger stood up from her

computer. "Good morning, everybody. Welcome to Friday, the beginning of the end of the chaos of the Winter Carnival. I overheard some of you talking about Saturday's snowmobile race, and I hope you will all be very careful. It is supposed to be a cold and snowy weekend."

Was Wittinger looking at him? Like she didn't trust him? Kelton had spent hours after school at the public library, watching snowmobiling videos, learning about safety and riding technique and emergency gear. He couldn't afford the fanciest, most expensive stuff, but he'd found pretty close substitutions. Nobody was more ready for the race than he was. Even if the rest of them didn't know it.

Just as long as that snowmobile belt was delivered today.

He held his hands over his belly as his stomach twisted from nerves or hunger.

"Today, we're going to begin a study of simple machines," said Mrs. Wittinger. "Most of the time, when we think of machines we envision, well, things like snowmobiles, with powerful engines and complex electrical systems. But in reality, that snowmobile consists of many smaller, simpler machines, the principles of which it is important to understand before we can succeed with larger machines."

Kelton moved forward a little in his seat. Finally, something interesting in science class.

Mrs. Wittinger continued. "So we'll be learning about simple machines which turn energy into work. Things like the inclined plane, the wheel and axle, the wedge, screw, lever, and pulley. And to help us learn about these things, we'll be doing some hands-on experiments. We'll do these with partners."

Kelton slumped in his seat, the excitement running out of him like water from a melting snowman. Working in partners was the worst. Sometimes the work wasn't so bad, but the choosing was always brutal.

"I want to give each of you the opportunity to work with someone you might not normally get to learn with, so I'll be assigning the partners," said Mrs. Wittinger. After a brief chorus of groans, she began reading off the names, and a minute later, Swann Siddiq sat down at his table with all her stuff. Kelton tried not to look at her, worried she'd catch him admiring her.

"Hey," she breathed. She offered him the same kind of tired, dismissive smile she had for most everything in McCall. Maybe some people would have found this insulting, but in a strange way Kelton found it encouraging. At least she didn't look down on him more than she did anyone else. It was a sad and pathetic attitude, he knew, but true nevertheless. From her depths of space-black hair, deep brown eyes, athletic frame, to her jeans and shirt so expensive that a lot of people hadn't even heard of the brands, Swann was beyond popular. She was a Super Popular. SuperPop.

And weirdly, she was kind of cool. After Mrs. Wittinger explained how they would measure different weights and levels of force with a pulley, a little ramp, and other things so basic he didn't think they should really be called machines, the two of them set to work. One time last year Kelton had been paired with McKenzie Crenner. She'd been stuck with him, and she'd left all the work to him. Swann was different. Instead of gabbing with her friends, she dug into the work with him, helping him find the answers for the lab worksheet. She wasn't even annoyed when he'd found a small mistake in her figures.

"Thanks," she said. "Nice catch. I hate getting little things wrong like that."

"No problem," he said. "I get ya." Kelton bit his lip. I get ya? Who says that? Just dorks.

"So you're pretty good at this kind of thing?" she asked. "I've heard you talking about fixing up a snowmobile? Getting it running?"

He felt as if he'd slipped through a portal into some kind of parallel universe. A different dimension where insanely beautiful girls asked him about his snowmobile.

"Yeah," he blurted out. "I mean, no. I wouldn't say I'm good at it. I have all these diagrams of the parts, and I've watched a ton of YouTube videos to figure out how to do most of it." His pencil lead broke as he was writing. Kelton breathed a curse. "Be right back." He went to the front of the room to sharpen his pencil.

As he cranked away at the sharpener, Mrs. Wittinger approached. "Hey, Kelton. How're you doing? How's your mom?"

Mrs. Wittinger and his mom had been friends back when they were in school together. They never talked now, but that didn't stop his teacher from asking questions like this, the way a lot of people asked questions about his mom, in a tone people usually saved for asking about someone who was really sick. It was a question laced with pity, and Kelton hated it. "Mom's fine." Cutting hair at Color & Cut and picking up extra shifts some nights at Bear Stone Brewery. She was fine.

When he turned back to his table, however, he was not fine. There was Swann, focused not on their work, but on his snowmobile binder, opened to his map page. "No, no, no," he whispered. If word of his plan got out, everybody would want to take his shortcut and he'd lose his advantage. So stupid, trusting a Popular. Should have been on guard, kept the binder closed. He hurried as best he could without looking like he was hurrying to close his binder.

"What was that?" Swann asked.

"Just a map," Kelton explained. "Nothing, really."

Swann watched him silently for a long moment. Kelton hated silences like this. Why couldn't he be like one of the cool guys, like Barrett or Bryden, the guys who always knew what to say?

"It's cool your dad's donating the snowmobile for a race prize. Did you get to hang out on the *Snowtastrophe III* set a lot? Did you ever ride the . . ."

He fell silent as he watched her tense up, her smile vanishing, as whatever tiny bit of connection the two of them had, froze colder than the Winter Carnival snow sculptures.

CHAPTER 2

AFTER SCHOOL, SWANN OPENED HER LOCKER TO FIND another folded piece of paper fluttering to the floor. Without hesitating for a moment, she calmly picked up the note and slipped it into her pocket. It was the third such note in as many weeks. She'd learned not to read them at her locker because the senders sometimes stood by, she guessed, to try to assess her reaction. One boy, Oakley, she thought his name was, had been really disappointed, she'd later learned, when she didn't smile after reading the part of his note that said something like, *I know we haven't known each other that long and maybe we don't know each other very good. But I really really really really like you, and I hope you like me too.*

Like him? This Oakley guy was probably really nice, but how could she like him if she didn't know him at all? She didn't want to hurt anyone else's feelings by not appearing happy or romantic enough after reading the note. She'd read it at home. Home. She sighed as she stuffed her books into her messenger bag.

"Oh, cool bag, Swann," Morgan Vaughn said, popping up

by her locker, running her fingers over the bag's leather. "What brand is it? Did you get this on Rodeo Drive? It's so cute."

"Thanks," Swann said, wishing now that she'd insisted on a simple canvas backpack from Target or someplace, something people wouldn't make a big deal about. "I think my mom gave me this bag for my birthday last year. I . . . don't know where she got it. Probably online."

"Oh my gosh, you are so lucky, Swann," Morgan said as the two of them headed for the front door and the parking lot. "I only get to go to the Boise Towne Square Mall maybe once a month."

McKenzie seemed to be waiting for them outside. Her words hit almost as sharply as the blast of February cold and the fresh wave of a new snowfall. "Swann, your babysitter's here!" Morgan started to protest, but McKenzie cut her off. "Oh, I'm sorry. Not babysitter. I mean your nanny."

Swann opened her mouth to explain, once again, that Cynthia was her au pair, but stopped. McKenzie wasn't half bad at sounding nice and sincere, but Swann knew she was just trying to get under her skin.

You think I don't understand this game? Swann thought, smiling at McKenzie. She could have dropped a line about how Cynthia had been hired to cook, clean, and drive Swann to and from school while her parents were away on a film shoot, but it was too easy a point scored, and Swann didn't even want to play the game. *The girls at my old school were masters at this kind of thing. They would have destroyed McKenzie, would have destroyed us both.*

Hunter Higgins emerged from the school with his cousin Yumi. Swann looked at him a moment, wondering if she should bother with what she thought she knew about Kelton Fielding and the race. *It's none of your business, and you don't even know Hunter,* she told herself. But that was the point, wasn't it? She basically knew nobody, and if she was stuck in this town, well . . . And she knew McCall and Idaho even less. Hunter had grown up here. His family had a cabin or something north of the lake, perhaps near the snowmobile racecourse. Maybe he could at least confirm what she'd thought she'd seen.

"Hey, Wolf Slayer," Swann said. Hunter looked surprised she was talking to him. She'd seen him protest sometimes when people had called him that, but her parents made a career out of understanding human expressions and she'd had some acting classes herself back home—back in L.A. Hunter didn't always hide his smile so well. He loved that nickname.

Hunter's cousin Yumi elbowed him and raised an eyebrow. If Yumi thought Swann wanted to talk to Hunter because she liked him, then Yumi was delusional.

"Hey, Swann, what's up?" Hunter asked.

Swann twisted her smile a little, the way she'd practiced in the mirror, a whimsical expression, her old acting teacher had called it. It let people know things weren't so serious, helped them relax. She gently touched his elbow, a simple friendly gesture she'd found always drew people's attention, especially boys. "It's probably nothing," she said, "but I've been thinking about the snowmobile race tomorrow, and I figured nobody knows that area of the woods as well as you. Your family has a cabin up there, right?"

Hunter smiled, and she knew she had him. "I wouldn't say I'm an expert. But I've been up there a few times."

Swann laughed. She could force a laugh with complete authenticity. "You mean a few times when you're up there shooting wolves and saving people." Now his cheeks turned red. Cynthia honked the Jeep's horn, and Swann held up a finger. "Look, I have to hurry, but in science today, I was partnered with Kelton Fielding."

Hunter rolled his eyes. "Sorry about that." Hunter reached out as though he were about to touch her shoulder, but then stopped himself. "Did he tap your shoulder every six seconds to get your attention?"

Swann shook her head. "Nothing like that. But he had this map out. One of those maps with all the lines to show elevation. A contour map? It looked like he had the course of the snowmobile race marked all around Mount McCall." She traced her finger around in a circle on her hand as though drawing the map there. "But then he's drawn a red line right over the mountain, like maybe there's a road up there?" She traced that line on her imaginary hand map.

Hunter thought for a moment. "It's an abandoned gold mine road." He looked at her with a mixture of shock and disgust.

"So you don't think I'm just imagining something or making a big deal out of nothing?"

"Kelton is . . ." Hunter folded his arms. "You don't know this guy. I've grown up with him. He doesn't care if he cheats. This last fall, he had no problem trespassing and illegally hunting with a salt block. He bragged about it, even. Now he's going to cheat at the race tomorrow."

Swann frowned. "Won't he be disqualified?"

Hunter looked away, gazing across the snowy parking lot as though he were thinking it all over. "I've never heard about a rule saying racers had to stay on the trail, but I don't think anyone's ever gone far off-trail. To even get on that road, he'd have to jump Stone Cold Gap, this place where there used to be a bridge over a creek. Kelton will be lucky to get his old snowmobile running. Making that jump? Forget it."

Cynthia honked the horn again. Swann shrugged. "Yeah, it sounds like he's just dreaming. I just wanted to make sure. Thanks, Hunter. I better go." She offered a little wave to the girls, to her friends, she guessed. "See you Monday," she said as she climbed up into the raised yellow Jeep four-by-four Mom and Dad had bought for Cynthia. The heat roared full-blast in the cab, just the way Swann liked it. "Thanks for cranking it," she said as she brushed snow from the sleeves of her coat. "I am still not used to this cold."

"You gotta embrace that chill, California!" Cynthia said. "It's only when you resist that it bothers you the worst."

Swann laughed a little. The first time Cynthia had called her "California," Swann had tried to correct her.

"Don't call me that!" she'd said.

Cynthia had laughed. "OK, California."

"Whatever, Country," Swann said now, even though Cynthia had a shiny stud piercing her nose and dressed more like the cool hiking-and-climbing-type from the cover of an outdoors magazine than a cowgirl and her sandy blond hair swept down around the left side of her face in a neat way. "I'm going to try to embrace it tomorrow. Provided you don't tell my dad and ruin my whole plan." She frowned as Cynthia turned onto a different street. "Where are we going?"

"Peggy from McCall Max Motorsports called," Cynthia said. "She says she has a sled for you to rent, but you have to put a credit card down for deposit tonight."

Swann leaned forward against her seat belt and threw a quick one-two air punch, imagining she was throwing her fists into Destiny's gut.

"You better not get me in trouble with this race."

Swann smiled. "Dad said he wouldn't buy me a snowmobile. He didn't say I couldn't rent one. He didn't say I couldn't enter the race."

The credit card Mom and Dad had provided was supposed to be for emergencies and incidentals only. When the two of them were away and Swann needed different shoes for some school activity or a book the school library didn't have, Swann could buy it in town or order it online. It would cost almost $300 to rent the snowmobile for the day, a little more to rent a helmet, snowmobile suit, boots, and gloves.

People said Winter Carnival drew thousands of tourists to town every year, and even though this was her first winter here,

Swann believed it. Two whole weeks were packed with all kinds of winter sports and party events. There were probably more snowmobiles than cars around town, and McCall Max Motorsports was packed with people renting machines and gear, as well as people talking about all of it. The more she learned of this snowmobiling activity, the less it seemed like a hobby or sport. These people treated it like a way of life.

It took almost forty-five minutes for Swann to finally find assistance getting fitted for gear. "You're the movie star's daughter?" Peggy asked.

Swann nodded, trying to maintain a cheerful look. "I'm Swann," she said uselessly.

Peggy nodded. "Your father is so kind, donating that snowmobile for a race prize. It's really generated a lot more interest in the sport. Lots of business for us. Be sure to thank him for me."

"Absolutely I will," Swann said. *If I ever get to talk to him.*

"I'll send the clothes and helmet home with you tonight," Peggy said. "You're welcome to come pick up the machine tomorrow, or, did you say this was for the race? We could drop it off at the starting area shortly before the three o'clock starting time."

"Sure," Swann said. "A drop-off for the race would be great."

"And I'll tell you what," Peggy said. "For Amir and Aurora Siddiq's daughter, ten percent discount."

Swann let out a long breath. Always about Amir and Aurora. "Wow," she said, forcing gratitude into her voice. "Thanks."

The snow fell even harder by the time they left the shop, and the Jeep's headlights cut through the swirl of snowflakes so that they seemed to light up like the many camera flashes from the tabloid people whenever they'd found her family somewhere in Hollywood.

After a few minutes heading north on Warren Wagon Road, Cynthia stopped the Jeep in one of several nature pull-over places.

"Is there something wrong?" Swann asked.

"Gonna put her in four-wheel drive. The snow is coming down faster than it has all day," she said. "Be great for snowmobiles tomorrow, but not so good for cars and trucks tonight." She whistled a little as she put the vehicle back in drive and returned to the highway. "January was already a record month for snow in McCall, and February is easily on course to break another record. I need to get up there skiing."

Swann hadn't known it was possible, but Cynthia was working on two college degrees at the same time. She was pursuing a master's degree in outdoor recreation so she could someday be a guide on trails or rivers and maybe work for the Forest or Park Service. She was also earning a master's degree in history, because, she said, she liked to learn about the great adventures of the past.

"Mind if we listen to my audiobook?" Cynthia said.

"More Magellan?" Swann asked. For the last two weeks, they'd listened to an audiobook about Ferdinand Magellan's expedition to sail a small fleet of ships all the way around the world. Incredible. Almost three hundred sailors had set out on the journey, and they'd had all kinds of problems.

"Nope," Cynthia answered. "Finished that on the drive to pick you up. Only nineteen of the sailors who started that mission survived."

"Nineteen?" Swann asked. "Is that even enough men to sail a ship?"

"They managed somehow," Cynthia said. "Nineteen starving sailors returned to Europe sailing from the opposite direction from which they'd left. Now I want to listen to this book about Ernest Shackleton and his mission to cross Antarctica. His ship, the *Endurance,* became stuck in the ice and they all almost died. It was a super-famous expedition."

"Almost died," Swann said. "So they lived. Why do you keep spoiling the ending?"

Cynthia adjusted her grip on the steering wheel as the Jeep fishtailed a little. "Because, California, the adventure is not in the ending, but in the journey."

"Clever. Did you get that from a postcard?"

Cynthia chuckled. "Probably, but that doesn't make it any less true. When I'm rock climbing, making an ascent up the mountain, the view from the top might be amazing, and there's an undeniable pride in having reached the summit. But the real fun is the climb itself. If not, I'd just drive or take a helicopter ride to the top. Skiing? The fun is all in the wild ride. Nobody is thrilled just because she's hanging around at the foot of the slope."

"OK." Swann held up her hands in surrender. "OK, I get it. Please. No more of your country wisdom."

Cynthia laughed again. "That's what I like about you, California. You give as good as you get."

The two of them stopped talking for the rest of the ride as the audiobook played. She listened as the narrator told them all about Ernest Shackleton's bold plan to cross all of Antarctica, crossing over the South Pole. By the time Cynthia rolled into her stall in the four-car garage at home, Shackleton's ship, the *Endurance,* was sailing farther and farther into the deep cold at the bottom of the world. It was one of those nights, like a lot of nights, when Swann wished the drive from school was longer, so they could listen to more of the story.

As she went inside, Swann tapped a preset button on her phone, and the lights all over the house gently adjusted, dimming or brightening exactly the way she liked it. It was a little brighter than her parents' normal setting, but Swann thought brighter was better, the light pushing away the lonely shadows a little.

"Earlier today, I made my famous goulash for supper." Cynthia shook her hands in mock alarm. Her voice echoed through the cathedral-ceilinged living room. "Sorry. For dinner. I figured a hearty pasta dish would give you plenty of energy for tomorrow's race. It won't take long for me to heat it up. Would you like it now, or do you want to knock out some homework first?"

Swann draped her coat over one of the twelve chairs around the long granite dining room table and tapped another control on her phone to light up the gas fireplace in the tall central brick column, the most prominent feature in the center of the room. "I thought Mom and Dad were supposed to be home."

"On a late flight."

Silence fell over the place, interrupted at irregular intervals only by the faint hiss and crackle of the fireplace.

"So eat now or later?" Cynthia said quietly.

If she ate now, she'd become too tired for homework. Best work while she was still sharp. "Later," she said.

"You got it," Cynthia said.

"I'll be in my library," said Swann. "I'll text you when I'm about ready."

Down the hall, past the ugly color-splotch abstract painting Mom had recently bought, past the double wood doors to the home theater, around the corner past the always closed and locked door to her parents' business office, beyond a shelf featuring several of her parents' awards, including an Oscar, past the big main stairs and down another hallway, Swann made her way to the back spiral staircase, the one that led up into the round rooms of the tower section on the corner of the house. Up on the third floor was the single greatest thing about moving to Idaho. Swann's library.

Dad, sensing she was disappointed by the idea of moving to this small town, had decided on his own to try to soften the blow by showing her the architect's sketches for converting this tower room to a haven for books.

She'd had to hold back tears when she'd first seen her new

library. Up by itself on the top floor of the tower, it was reached by a spiral staircase, leaving all four walls, save for four window seats with amazing views of the woods and of Lake Payette, completely devoted to bookshelf space. She had a small desk up there, but Swann did most of her homework in her very favorite spot, a padded wicker shell chair hanging from the ceiling. Wrapped in a quilt inside the hanging basket, Swann could relax. She could almost forget that her home and parents were a thousand miles away. She almost didn't notice the heavy quiet in the nearly empty house.

CHAPTER 3

KELTON FIELDING WASN'T ONE OF THOSE NERDY KIDS WHO spent forever around school at the end of the day. He didn't have anything else to say to the teachers, and he knew from experience that hanging out on the playground after the last bell was a great way to get beat up. But that Friday, Kelton had an even stronger need to get out of there as fast as he could.

The part. The part. The part. That afternoon, Ms. Foudy, his English and homeroom teacher, had warned him to pay attention. She'd been griping about that all week, but how could he be expected to care about some stupid poem about chickens and a wheelbarrow when everything depended on the arrival of this belt for his snowmobile? It had taken him over eight months to get the machine's engine running, but without that belt, the thing wouldn't actually move. He needed that belt so he could win the race. Not just because he wanted to show up all the people who'd made fun of him about his broken-down sled, but because the sale of the super-duper prize sled might help make sure his family didn't have to move again, and if they could stay in the house they were renting now, Kelton just might be able to get Scruffy. Maybe the mean old man would sell the dog.

Passing by Eagle Pawn Shop, Kelton looked through the window to a shelf halfway back in the cluttered shop. He did this every day, and so far, every day he was relieved to see Steve's prized possession still hadn't been sold. It was a World War II German dagger with a skull and evil swastika carved into the steel handle. Steve said his great-grandfather had taken it off a dead Nazi during the war and had handed it down until he got it. The pawnshop owner had given Kelton $200 for the knife. As soon as he won the snowmobile race and scored his money, he'd have to shell out $250 to purchase the blade and return it to the box at the back of Steve's closet. Everything would be fine. As long as that belt had been delivered.

The sun was low in the west by the time he reached the rickety fence near the dilapidated trailer where Scruffy lived. The dog had barked a little but stopped as soon as he got a good sniff of Kelton. Kelton reached through the fence and petted his matted damp fur. "Oh, you're so cold, buddy. You gotta stay in your doghouse tonight, try to get out of this snow."

Scruffy licked Kelton's fingers while he wagged his tail. Kelton laughed. "Sorry, pal. I don't have nothing for you."

The little dog whined.

Kelton sighed. "Well, OK. I'll try harder next time. It's not easy, though. We're not allowed to take food out of the cafeteria, and, like today, it's hard to smuggle out chicken and noodles and green beans." He scratched behind the dog's ears the way he knew the pup just loved. "Now I have to get going, but I'll make you a deal. I win this race tomorrow, I'll buy a big sack of dog food, be able to feed you better for a long time. Maybe I'll get you some of that canned meat type of dog food. I've seen that stuff before. Some of it looks good enough for people to eat. Bet you'd love it."

Kelton stood up and took a few steps away. The dog whined. "I'm sorry, buddy. I have to go. If that belt's here, I have a ton of work to do." He started jogging off through the thick snow. "If the belt's not here . . ."

He didn't want to think about that.

A few blocks more, forgetting about trying to run through shoveled areas or through his old tracks, Kelton's feet were freezing, his shoes full of snow. At last, he skidded to a halt near the mailbox in front of his house. He placed his hand on the little metal loop thing at the top of the mailbox door and pulled.

"Yes!" A cardboard box. But was it the right one? He yanked it from the mailbox, shoving the SECOND NOTICE bill envelopes back inside. There was still enough light out to read . . . " 'Kelton Fielding'! Yes!"

The box was addressed to him. It was the right weight. The right shape. He rushed up the snow-covered sidewalk and path to the house. The lights weren't on inside and the door was locked, so he bent down to pull the spare key from the hole in the rotted part of the door-trim board.

Inside, he was careful to remove his shoes and brush off any extra snow from around his ankles onto the front rug so that

Steve wouldn't yell at him again about water being all over the floor. In the kitchen, he found a knife to help him cut the tape and open the box.

At last, he held the thing in his hands, that long loop of thick black rubber. It was finally real, but he had been dreaming about it, trying to figure out a way to get it, for so long that a part of him struggled to believe he really had it.

He carefully placed it on the kitchen counter so he could grab a clean glass to get a drink, and that was when he found the note. In this house, people had school and worked at odd hours. (Well, mostly he and Mom went to school or worked. Steve was still looking for a job.) So a lot of communication happened by notes.

KEL,

X-TRA SHIFT AT BEAR STONE 2NITE. LAST FRIDAY OF CARNIVAL. HOPE FOR BIG TIPS! BE HOME LATE. STEVE WILL FIX YOU A FROZEN PIZZA. LOVE YOU MORE THAN ALL THE SNOWFLAKES OUT THERE TODAY.

MOM

A quick survey of the house, and the fact that Steve's 1987 Chevy Monte Carlo SS wasn't in the driveway, told him he was on his own for frozen pizza. He smiled and turned the oven dial to 450. A twelve-year-old didn't spend this much time alone without figuring out how to cook for himself. He was a master chef with the fro-pi.

Less than an hour later, he took his snowmobile belt and two slices of Tombstone pepperoni out to the garage. There it was. His red 2006 Ski-Doo Summit 800. He squeezed the belt in his hands. "Hey there. You ready to get to work? We got a race to win tomorrow."

Kelton shivered. This garage wasn't special. It was filled with all kinds of old junk, but the one thing it had going for it was this big electric heater Steve had installed last year when he was working out here installing new rims and a cherry-bomb glass pack on his Monte Carlo. Mom hated when anyone ran the heater, said it cranked up the electric bill. But how much extra could it cost? Kelton could pay her back the difference from his race winnings. He turned the dial, firing up the heat, and took a bite of his fro-pi. He sat down on the back bench seat that Steve had been promising to put back into Mom's minivan ever since he used her vehicle to haul a bunch of old scrap lumber for one of his friends.

Kelton was glad the bench hadn't been put back yet. It was handy for when he worked out here. When he was finished with supper, he wiped the grease on his jeans and then grabbed the belt to go to work. He already had the left-side engine cover off, the tool kit out, the belt guard removed, and the tension on the secondary clutch relaxed. He'd done it weeks ago, just like the guy on the YouTube video he'd watched at the library. It was a lot easier than he'd thought it would be.

Now he checked the new belt to make sure the arrows on it were pointing toward the front of the sled. Gritting his teeth in concentration, hoping he didn't mess this up somehow, he looped the belt around the circular metal-drum-like primary clutch before easing it over the metal lip of the round secondary clutch.

"Kind of easy so far," he said to his sled, patting the seat when he had the belt on. For just a moment he felt a spike of panic when he couldn't find the clutch adjustment tool that came in the Ski-Doo tool kit, but he relaxed when he found it on the workbench. "Don't worry," he assured his snowmobile. "From now on, I'll put all the tools back in the onboard compartment as soon as I'm done with them." If he'd have lost that tool, it would have been all over. He slipped the end of the tool into the hole on the secondary clutch and rotated it counterclockwise to tighten the clutch and seat the belt.

"Piece of cake," Kelton said. He carefully returned the tool to the black pouch that came with the snowmobile and strapped it back into its compartment near the bottom of the secondary clutch.

In the maintenance video he'd watched, the guy talked about how he liked to have a couple of his friends help him with the next part, pushing the snowmobile back and forth to move the track and therefore the clutch and belt, the better to make sure the belt was fully seated. This was going to be tough. Nobody was around, and even if Steve was home, he probably wouldn't help.

Kelton crouched down behind the sled, took a deep breath, and pushed hard, driving his legs, grunting. "Come . . . on." It moved forward an inch, two inches, six inches. He stopped, went around to the front of the sled, and pushed it back. Then he reinstalled the belt guard and closed the machine.

"And that . . . is it," he said.

Could it be true? After working, sweating, dreaming about getting his snowmobile running and working again, could it be ready? He smiled. "There's only one way to find out."

Kelton suited up. He didn't own a nice once-piece regular snowmobile suit. Instead he put on a pair of overalls-with-suspenders-style snow pants, his old snow boots, which ran a little small, two sweatshirts, a coat, and a big waterproof light coat that had belonged to Darren. A pair of gloves and Darren's old helmet completed his gear. He didn't look like a pro, but he hoped he'd stay warm and dry. Even on a warmer snowmobile day, with temperatures near or even slightly above freezing, once a rider cranked up the speed on his sled, once he was out there charging through snow, especially wet snow, he could get cold very fast. Kelton had watched YouTube snowmobiling videos about frostbite. Horrible stuff.

He heaved open the garage door, shoving hard to get it to snap beyond its regular sticking point. The cold blast and wave of snow stung his cheeks at once, but he smiled, realizing the rest of him felt perfectly comfortable, a little warm even, and his face and ears would be fine once the helmet was on. He pushed it down over his head, a good fit. Then with another huge effort, he dragged the snowmobile backward. He didn't have one of those fancy sleds that actually had a reverse gear.

"Yes," he hissed. "That's the way. Nice and easy."

Out in the snow, he positioned his snowmobile just right, and then yanked the pull start to fire it up. It roared to life in one pull! It was working! For so long now, he'd been telling people about how he was right on the edge of getting this snowmobile to run, to work, and now he'd done it. He, Kelton, working out of this junked garage all by himself, had taken this expensive broken machine and figured out how to make it run and work again. He felt the vibration of its motor, of the sled's power, shaking up through his hands, and it felt like his power. He had made this happen when guys like Bryden Simmons and Richie Hunter Higgins thought he'd never be able to do it.

As soon as his sled eased out onto the blanket of thick white snow it glided smoothly, almost as if it were floating on water. And then the moment toward which he had been working for many months had arrived. It was time to ride. Throwing his leg over the sled, he sat down behind its handlebars and flicked on the headlight to shine a beam through the heavy sparkle of snowfall. Then he eased on the throttle. Not too much. He'd warm it up in the vacant lot behind the garage, take a few laps to let that belt get seated right, just like the guy on the video said.

Gliding out into the snowy back lot, his snowmobile ran perfectly, and Kelton laughed with joy. His sled was old, but he'd learned a lot, worked hard, and fixed it up good as new. He sped up a little as he cleared the shrubbery near the garage. His sled shot ahead so easily, with so much power and instant speed even as he barely hit the throttle. What would it feel like when he took it up to full power?

Back in this lot, there were a couple of bumps, rocks, and old leaf piles, plus places where Steve dumped the grass clippings when he mowed. The thick powder covered all that now and Kelton's Ski-Doo bobbed over it all. Turning the handlebars, Kelton eased his sled into a wide curve at the end of the lot, slowly enough that he didn't even need to lean against the turn for balance.

Perfect. He reached back a hand to slap the seat behind him, the way a cowboy might swat his horse to put on more speed, and he throttled up. "Come on," he said inside his helmet. "Let's pick it up a little."

The sled obeyed, and instantly shot ahead faster. He laughed, remembering riding with Darren on the trails outside of town. Oh, they had gone fast, trees and shrubbery beside them melting into a blur as they shot through the snow. Darren had even let him take the controls, trusting him, even though he was so young, and he'd laughed when Kelton had shouted and buried the throttle right away.

"There you go!" Darren had said, and laughed. He patted Kelton's back, squeezed his shoulder. "Crank it up! You feel the need for speed! You're a natural at this, kid. A pro already."

Nobody else ever said those kinds of things about him, cheered him on like that. Mom and Darren had broken up more than three years ago, but zipping around on this snowmobile now, it felt that hardly any time had passed at all.

The two of them had enjoyed that 2006 Ski-Doo Summit 800 for weeks. But eventually the snowmobile had trouble and wouldn't run.

Then one morning, after a night with a lot of shouting and slamming doors, Darren was gone, the snowmobile broken down and forgotten in the back corner of the garage.

Until now. Now it rode again, power, grace, and speed, and he had made it happen. He rode the snowmobile around and around that lot for about a half hour, taking it easy on the throttle, but eager to open it up tomorrow in the race.

Finally, he patted it atop the handlebars. "That's it for tonight. Gas ain't free."

He drove back to park in the garage and shut down the engine before filling its fuel tank, ready for tomorrow's race. Steve still wasn't home, even though it was getting pretty late. That wasn't all that unusual.

"Suppose I should go back inside," Kelton said aloud. He also supposed he shouldn't talk to himself so much. To anyone else, he'd seem like a crazy person, but being alone as much as he was, the quiet got to him. "At least nobody's around to make fun of me about it."

Instead of going into the boring empty house, he remained in the garage, practicing, as he had countless times before, different positions and leans on the sled, useful for traversing high snowy slopes or for getting the snowmobile unstuck in thick snow. It would have been better if he could have practiced out on actual slopes, but he hadn't had that luxury. A guy like Hunter Higgins could take out his family's fancy newer snowmobile whenever he wanted, November through March, could get all the practice he needed. People like that had no idea how lucky they were, perfect families and everything handed to them. "Bet they never even go off the trail," Kelton said.

He opened his snowmobile binder and reviewed his shortcut map just to be certain he knew the way. With that route, and everything he'd learned from the snowmobile pro YouTube videos, plus all his practice in the garage, he had a solid chance to win tomorrow's race.

He settled down on the back bench seat from Mom's minivan, comfortable with the warm breeze from the droning heater washing over him. And he closed his eyes for just a moment.

A BLAST OF COLD AIR AND THE ROAR OF A LOUD SQUEAKY engine jolted him awake. Kelton sat straight up, blinking, bright headlights blinding him. "What's going on?"

Mom's minivan was parked outside the garage, snow still coming down. "Kelton! What are you doing out here?" She jumped back into her vehicle and drove into the garage. She shut off the minivan lights and revved the engine a little. Kelton knew that inside the vehicle she'd also turned off the radio and heater. She was revving it, the better to charge the battery so the van would start next time. Leaving any of the electrical stuff on when shutting off the engine was just asking for a jump start next time she had to go somewhere.

"Were you sleeping out here?" Mom shouted when she got out of the van. She slammed the driver's-side door. "What are you doing? It's after midnight! Where's Steve? What did I tell you about running that heater, Kelton?" She cursed, spinning the control dial to shut the heater off. "Electric bill will be through the roof! Get inside! Where's Steve?"

"I don't know!" Kelton said. "I'm sorry. I just dozed off. I didn't mean to run the heater that long."

"Don't run that heater at all, Kelton!" Mom snapped, checking her cell phone. She started tapping the screen, probably texting Steve. "There's no reason for you to be out here to need that heater! Get inside! Go to bed."

Kelton didn't argue. Arguing with Mom never got him anywhere anyway, especially when she was this mad. Kelton rushed inside to his room, shut the door, changed into his old Iron Man pajamas, and dropped under the cold blankets. He shivered there, waiting for his bed to warm up, and was asleep after a few minutes.

Some time later, he heard the expected shouting, the cursing, the slamming doors.

"Where were you? You were supposed to take care of Kelton!"

"It's Winter Carnival! I was out with Trevor and the guys. That kid can take care of himself!"

"Trevor and the guys! Trevor and the guys! It's always Trevor and the guys. It's never a job! Never looking out for Kelton! Just you and that stupid old Monte Carlo you can't afford, out spending money we don't have!"

"That car is an American classic, Josie!"

Fights like this weren't uncommon, but lately they were louder, longer, and more frequent. This went on for a long time, until, at last, Mom took the final step. "Out! Get out! We're done! Take your stupid Monte Crapo and leave! I'll drop the rest of your junk at Trevor's! Get out!"

"Fine!"

"Fine!"

More swearing.

"I don't need this!"

"Fine!"

And after the final slamming door, the little house fell silent, save for the sound of his mother's sniffles and quiet sobs.

"Don't worry, Mom," Kelton whispered to himself beneath his blankets. "I'll win that race tomorrow, sell that fancy custom snowmobile for a pile of money, and then you and me and maybe Scruffy will be fine. We'll be fine, Mom. For real."

CHAPTER 4

THE NEXT DAY MOM WAS OFF TO WORK, AND STEVE WAS still gone. No big loss there. Except when it came to working on his old Monte Carlo, he was kind of lazy. And he got mad a lot. The bigger problem Kelton had now was that stupid knife.

The thing had sat in an old wooden cigar box at the back of the closet. Steve had only shown it to Kelton that one time when he moved in. Then it was kind of forgotten. But if Mom was going to move all Steve's stuff over to Trevor's, maybe that cigar box would be on top of the pile. Maybe Steve would look inside it while he had it out. And if that happened, he'd know Kelton had taken the knife.

Borrowed the knife, really.

OK. Maybe he'd stolen the knife. He hated stealing. It made him feel like a real scumbag, as though the things people said about him and his mom were true.

Worrying about it all made Saturday drag on forever. McCall's snowmobile race used to start in the morning, but it had been revised so that it started later in the day when it was slightly warmer. But what difference did it really make, when all the racers were packed into cold-weather gear anyway? Kelton just needed to get out there, win the race, and get the knife back. It all would have been a lot easier if Steve hadn't had a big fight with Mom and gotten himself kicked out.

After the longest wait in his life, a Saturday spent checking and rechecking his gear and snowmobile, a day when he didn't eat nothing because he was so nervous, it was finally time to get ready and get to the race. Suited up, with one extra sweatshirt added to the two already beneath his outer waterproof jacket, he sat down for a moment on his snowmobile.

Kelton reached over and tugged the five-foot pole that held up his orange safety flag. It was required by McCall law when riding in town. He'd checked the regs on the city website. A snowmobiler wasn't allowed to ride in town except directly from his house to the gas station or to the trailheads outside of town.

That orange flag reminded him of one of the most important things he'd figured out in life. There were three kinds of people in the world. You had the Populars—the Pops—who were usually also Richies, people who had everything handed to them and never had a problem their mommies and daddies wouldn't fix. Then there were the Grits, people who had nothing going for them, poor people with no advantages, no breaks, and they whined about it like they were helpless, like, *Oh, boo-hoo! Life ain't fair so I'm just gonna sit on the couch and eat chips the rest of my life.* The more he thought about it, the more he figured Steve was one of those helpless kind of Grits. But there was a third kind of person, the Fighter Grits. This type of Grit was poor and barely had any chance, but still fought back. Like, a lot of the teachers thought Kelton would never do anything good. But, thing was, what they didn't know was Kelton was more a Fighter Grit, a guy who bent the rules sometimes, as long as he didn't hurt anybody, to get ahead of—no, to finally catch up with—the Richies and the Populars.

So he'd temporarily stolen a knife so he could pay for his snowmobile registration, the belt, and the race entry fee. Now he'd bend the rules again. He'd read the Idaho and McCall snowmobile regulations websites over and over again. He'd even asked the librarian if he understood the rules right, and she agreed with him. The state of Idaho recommended that people under sixteen ride with an adult. Recommended, but not required. The city of McCall said a rider had to have a driver's license to ride a snowmobile in town, requiring that riders be at least sixteen. It wouldn't be a problem for Pops like Hunter Higgins or Bryden Simmons, whose parents would either cart their sleds on a trailer down to the trailhead outside the city limits or would drive the snowmobiles down there themselves before turning them over to their kids. Kelton had neither a snowmobile trailer nor a parent willing to drive the sled to the trailhead. How was that his fault? What had he done wrong to not technically be allowed to drive his snowmobile to the start of the race?

Nothing. But Kelton wouldn't sit around like Steve, endlessly complaining about life being unfair. He'd only be bending the city law a little bit while he drove his snowmobile across town and up Warren Wagon Road to the start of the race. He knew and would obey all the traffic laws. Nobody would get hurt. And when he was wearing all his gear, nobody would even know the rider of his snowmobile was under sixteen and didn't have a license.

Kelton pull-started his snowmobile and laughed a little when it fired up on the first crank. "Yeah, nobody's doing me any favors," he said quietly. "Gotta take every chance I can get." Like his shortcut overpass in the race. A little risky, maybe, but he wasn't chicken. And for once, Kelton Fielding was going to come out on top. For real.

He slipped on his helmet and dragged his sled out of the garage. The snow was even thicker now than it had been last night. It hadn't snowed all day, but a big snowstorm was forecast for the overnight, and already the first few gentle flakes were falling. He shut the garage, hopped back on his sled, and then glided down his driveway, heading toward the race.

"ONE HALF-CAFF, NO-FOAM, EXTRA-HOT, EXTRA-SWEET, nonfat caramel mocha," Cynthia said, handing the large white paper cup to Swann.

Swann smiled, surveying the parking lot that would serve as the starting point for the snowmobile race. Peggy at Max Motorsports had the machine hauled down, gassed up, and ready. "With whip?"

Cynthia nodded. "Whip and a drizzle of caramel on top."

Swann took the black plastic lid off. She never liked sipping through the tiny hole. That was always a gamble. When is the hot coffee going to hit your lips? How far back do you have to tip it before the coffee comes out? Will it be too hot to drink? She'd spare herself the surprise and the possible minor injury by just popping the lid off. "No double cup?"

Cynthia sighed. She was usually pretty patient with Swann, but she had her limits. "It's a small town, Swann. No Starbucks here. Sharlie's Coffee Shop won't double-cup."

Swann was about to sigh and roll her eyes, but she stopped herself, smiling instead. Sharlie was the name of the lake monster that legend said swam the depths of Lake Payette on the north side of McCall. Cynthia must have noticed Swann's self-control, because she grinned, sipping what was no doubt her normal plain black coffee. Cowboy coffee, she always called it. Cynthia knew of Swann's determination to avoid becoming the spoiled-rich-girl-moved-to-a-small-town character like the one from the Hallmark Christmas movie *Back to the Hometown Christmas,* in which Swann's mother had starred.

More and more snowmobiles slid down from Warren Wagon Road to the starting line in the parking lot. Bryden Simmons was all set up with his super-good snowmobile from his parents' shop. His family had arrived really early, bringing out a few rental machines, so he had secured a great position for his snowmobile up near the starting line.

Swann pulled out her phone and took a few photos of the machines lining up for the race. If Margo, her parents' publicist, said the shots were OK, she'd post them to her FriendStar account.

Bryden spotted her and did that thing where he looked at her, but then looked away, and then started to approach her, but then acted like he wasn't thinking about approaching. She'd seen this a lot before, from different boys, especially here in McCall. She only hoped he wasn't going to ask her to go with him to the winter dance or to a party. She wasn't going to commit to something like that, at least not out here in front of everyone.

Finally Bryden stepped up. "Oh, hi there, Swann. You, um, is that . . . you got a coffee there?"

Swann smiled, trying to help the guy, so he wouldn't feel so horribly uncomfortable. "Yeah, a mocha."

"Ah," Bryden said. "That's good. You got the, um, the snowmobile. Mom said you'd ordered, you know, rented it. That's good." He shifted his weight. "Is it, you know, good?"

Swann grinned. "Oh yeah, Bryden. It's great. Thanks." One thing Swann had learned about junior high boys was that what they liked to talk about most was themselves. Clearly, Bryden was miserable with whatever he was trying to do, so she'd help him out. "What kind of snowmobile do you have? Is it a good one?"

The veil of awkwardness was lifted from him, and his coolness she'd seen in him before returned. "Oh yeah! It's a Polaris 850 Switchback Assault. A pretty awesome machine. My dad says if I'm going to be out shredding powder, I need to represent the shop, so I usually go with a pretty great sled. This one's only a couple years old. What's great about the Polaris 850 . . ."

Swann nodded as though she were still listening, sipping her drink. Not that what he was saying wasn't interesting. She just didn't want to hear quite that much information right at that moment. He seemed happier talking about it, though.

A truck pulled up, and Hunter and Yumi Higgins worked with some men to unload a snowmobile from a trailer. Hunter and Yumi. Those two were always together. "Must be nice," Swann said quietly. She supposed she was with Cynthia even more than the Higgins cousins hung out, but Cynthia didn't count, being like fifteen years older and paid to be there.

Hunter talked to the men a little, and they patted his shoulder, bumped fists, and did other things boys and men did when about to begin a sports contest. Then he rode ahead slowly, Yumi walking at his side.

"Hey, Swann!" Hunter called when he saw her. He slid to a stop next to her. "So you decided to do the race after all. Cool."

Swann held up her helmet, ready to slip it on in a moment. She looked over the crowded parking lot. "Shh." She leaned closer to Hunter. "My parents might be around here somewhere. They don't know I'm racing. I'm trying to keep it a surprise." Before either of them could ask questions about that, Swann turned to Yumi. "Not racing?"

Yumi shrugged. "Not really my thing. I go out on the snowmobiles once in a while but not in a race. Anyway, I prefer skiing or sledding."

"Oh, do you ski?" Swann asked, happily surprised.

Yumi swung her arm in a sweeping gesture. "It's McCall. The outdoors is what we do. Of course I ski."

Swann and Yumi hadn't talked much. Swann hadn't been in volleyball or basketball with her, and there wasn't much time to talk between classes. Yet still Swann noticed the stand-off attitude, the hostility toward her, Swann the outsider, Swann the rich girl. This was one of the several reasons Swann worked to try to avoid seeming like that character.

"Cool. Maybe we could go skiing together?" Swann tried. "My parents and I have gone skiing a few times, but I'm not that good. Maybe you can offer me some pointers."

Yumi flashed a strange expression, like a reluctant smile. "Yeah," she said. "Maybe."

More snowmobiles came down off the road. It would be a crowded race. Finally, Swann spotted one of the newcomers riding to a halt among the racers and taking off his helmet. Kelton Fielding.

Hunter must have followed her gaze, because he frowned when he saw Kelton. "I'm going to try to move my snowmobile up a little."

"Higgins, just let it go," Yumi said quietly, stepping closer to Hunter. "It's stupid."

"No, I'm not going to let him cheat," Hunter said.

"It's not against the rules," Yumi replied. "He's not cheating."

"It's the spirit of the thing," Hunter said. "I'm not letting him win that way."

Swann stepped up to the two of them, downing the last of her mocha. "You might want to keep it down. The more people hear about Kelton's shortcut, the more will try to take it themselves."

"You're going to take it?" Yumi asked.

Swann shrugged. "It seems like the best way to win. And like Hunter said. Better me than Kelton."

"That's not what he said," Yumi offered.

Swann smiled at Hunter. "You do what you want. I'm taking the shortcut."

An air horn pierced the air, and then a familiar voice came over a bullhorn.

Good afternoon, racers! Good afternoon!

Swann shoved her helmet on as her father and mother climbed up onto the bed of a pickup truck. People applauded wildly as soon as they realized who was speaking. Dad was wearing jeans and a plaid shirt with an open puffy jacket, new stuff he'd bought to look rustic and try to fit in around McCall. Mom had a super-cool new snowmobile outfit with pink trim lines and pink snow boots. They both smiled warmly.

I'm Amir Siddiq. You may have seen me, and a certain fantastic snowmobile, in the hit action movie Snowtastrophe III.

People cheered. *Snowtastrophe III* had been an even bigger hit than the first two movies in the franchise.

Swann's mom took the bullhorn.

I'm Aurora Siddiq. We're so happy to be here.

She returned the bullhorn to Dad and he put his arm around her as he spoke.

Aurora and I absolutely love it in McCall. You all have been so welcoming and kind. This is the best place on earth. And when I heard there was going to be a Winter Carnival and a snowmobile race, I wanted to say thank you. That's why I'm donating, in addition to the regular annual five-hundred-dollar cash prize, my customized Yamaha Sidewinder SRX LE snowmobile, the actual machine that my character used in Snowtastrophe III.

People applauded. The clapping sounded strange, muffled as it was by gloves. Swann clapped to blend in.

Now, this snowmobile doesn't actually fire high-powered, weaponized lasers. Those are illegal, even in gun-friendly Idaho, and more importantly, the laser blasts were actually added by the wizards in the computer effects department. But it does have some cool lights, and it is, absolutely, fast.

Dad laughed.

Seriously. I was able to tear the thing away from my stunt double a couple of times, and the thing just tears up the snow. It's like a rocket!

Her parents were so cool. So kind and so much fun. It's just that they'd moved the family home to Idaho, but the family business remained in California. They were gone all the time. There were her parents warming a crowd and, although she knew they had to do what they did for a living and she'd never ask them to do otherwise, she only wished she had a little more of their fun warmth for herself.

A woman from the McCall Area Snowmobile Club thanked

Swann's dad and reminded everyone of the rules. No sled-on-sled contact. All racers must check in at all race checkpoints for safety. All racers must wear helmets, an unnecessary rule since the cold alone made all riders sure to wear a full helmet. No alcohol could be consumed during the race. Pretty basic stuff. After that, racers were asked to mount up and start their sleds. Swann had a good position, about two sled lengths back behind Kelton, eyes on his red machine and maroon jacket. In a matter of seconds the race would begin.

ON ONE OF THE SNOWMOBILING YOUTUBE VIDEOS KELTON had watched, the pro who was offering all the riding tips started with Rule 1: Don't Forget to Breathe. Watching it, Kelton had thought it was the dumbest thing. He'd figured it was physically impossible to forget to breathe. Even an unconscious guy kept breathing.

Yet now, in the seconds before the starting pistol signaled the beginning of the race, he understood. His muscles tense, he gripped his handlebars tight, ready to blip the throttle and pour on the speed. But he wouldn't crank it full blast. Everybody else could shoot ahead into a big cluster, bumping into each other, hitting the brakes, trying to get clear. He'd let the crowd jump ahead, and then spot his way around.

With his shortcut, he didn't need to be in the lead. He was going to bypass a major portion of the racecourse. Straight through checkpoint one, up over the gold mine pass, and right down to checkpoint two ahead of everyone else. Then it would be a wide-open trail for him to speed along at a good pace, safe from anyone else's interference. In a little more than an hour, he'd own the coolest snowmobile in America.

The starting pistol fired, and he blipped the throttle, revving it up to get it going, but then hanging back for a moment while the rest of the herd surged into a giant knot of snowmobiles ahead of him.

"Breathe!" he said quietly to himself inside his helmet. "On the left!" There was a space to shoot through if he really gunned it. Kelton sped up his sled, riding for all he was worth to squeeze through the tiny, single-snowmobile space on the left side. "Come on, come on, come on!" One guy on a blue snowmobile ahead of Kelton looked like he was steering for the outside too.

"Don't do it!" Kelton shouted, even though he knew nobody could hear him through his helmet and out here in the roar from all the snowmobiles. "Come on!" he called to his own sled. "You can do it!"

With inches to spare, Kelton shot through the gap and glided into a great position in the center of the trail, just a few lengths behind the half-dozen sleds leading the race.

Now he blazed ahead, risking a quick look at the pack behind him. His snowmobile raced down the well-groomed and packed trail, flying across the white, through a sort of tunnel formed by the tree branches overhead.

It was happening! He was way out near the front, and with his super-time-saving shortcut still to come. The race was his.

His sled was running great. He could feel its power, like it was hungry, tearing at the snow, its track biting solid and throwing the machine over the white faster and faster.

Kelton rode like that, mostly on a straightaway, but taking a few small curves, careful to always hug the inside of them, to take as straight a path as possible. The speed was fantastic. Several times he laughed at the delight of it all. Everything flew by in a blur, like this whole amazing day was a dream, like he'd fallen asleep on that bench seat in the garage near his snowmobile last night and at any moment he could wake up from this. But then his snowmobile would shoot up over a little bump, flipping his stomach with that split second of weightlessness, like when a roller coaster whips up over a sharp hill, and he knew more than at any other time that he was awake, and more alive than he'd ever been before.

He peered through the light mist that the lead snowmobiles kicked up in their wake. Seven, maybe eight machines ahead of him. And beyond them, barely visible, was it? Yes! Orange flags on tall poles on either side of the trail! Checkpoint one, coming up about a hundred, hundred fifty yards ahead. About a half mile after that was the turnoff trail for his shortcut.

"Maybe just stay on the main course," Kelton said inside his helmet. "You're only in ninth place or something. Maybe just ride the whole thing and try to pass them."

But even as he said it, he knew that was crap. The leaders were probably Richies on the fastest sleds out there. Hard to tell with the gear and helmets, but he was pretty sure that was

Bryden Simmons on his charged Polaris up there. Thing was, this race, like all of life, wasn't an example of fairness. No. The shortcut was his only chance to even things out. It meant for a slightly tougher run through deeper powder, but he could do it. He patted his snowmobile. "You ready for this?" Suddenly he was through the first checkpoint and watching intensely for his secret turn.

"Come on. Where are you?" Kelton said to himself. The turnoff was easy to see on the map. But maps aren't real life. No rock outcroppings on a map. On a map, the trees didn't block one's view like they did in real life. His shortcut wasn't part of the county's well-maintained trail system. It might be quite overgrown, hard to spot. And there were lots of side trails off the main route. How could he know which was his shortcut? On the map, his pass wound up between the Big and Little McCall peaks, but it was hard to see the mountains down in the woods. Maybe he should have checked the distance on the map, tried to measure how far he'd gone beyond the checkpoint.

Kelton kept glancing to his right, trying to spot the high valley between the two peaks, looking for a clearing or even a trace of the road. Finally, the woods thinned out a little as the trail ran slightly closer to a distant creek. Was this it? Coming up on his right?

"It has to be." He knew he'd eventually have to risk trying one of these side trails, hoping it was the right one. If he was wrong, he'd lose the race. There would be no second chance. He could try one of the offshoots, hoping it was his shortcut, and maybe win the race. Or he could chicken out, not try, and lose the race for sure.

He was tired of being the outcast, the last picked, the unseen, forgotten one. Just this once, he would finally do something right, finally get something besides the worst of everything, finally . . . win! He cranked his snowmobile hard to the right, leaning in that direction to center himself as he skidded around a tight turn, and an instant later he was flying ahead through much looser powder. He squeezed the throttle to give the sled the extra power it needed, and it bucked ahead over the uneven snow. Other snowmobiles had taken this path a while back, because compared to the snow on either side, the trail was kind of packed down, but this route hadn't been used since the most recent heavy snowfalls.

There was just one way to know if he'd taken the right path. A long time ago, train tracks ran up the pass to the gold mine, with a railroad bridge over a stream. The tracks and bridge were long gone, but if he was running their former path right now, there should be a little rise before the creek. These days people called it Stone Cold Gap, Kelton guessed because any snowmobiler crazy enough to try to jump over the creek had to have stone-cold nerves. He slowed down as his rough trail rose up a little slope, and he hit the brakes hard, skidding to a halt, his heart leaping for a moment as he worried he was about to spill forward into the freezing stream below.

Kelton took off his helmet for just a moment, the icy sting

of the winter air a welcome change from the tense heat inside. "Stone Cold Gap." He smiled. He'd found the right trail after all. Now he'd turn around, go back to give himself a running start, and then, if his courage held, he'd gun it full speed for the most intense snowmobile jump of his life.

CHAPTER 5

SWANN HAD SEEN *SNOWTASTROPHE III* A BUNCH OF times, including special private premiere screenings in New York and London. She'd always been impressed by the racing snowmobile battle scenes high in the snowcapped mountains. In the movie, her dad, his stunt double, and the special effects team made high-speed snowmobile racing look easy. It was not easy. She wasn't sure what she was doing wrong, but snowmobiles shot past her right and left one after another, while she just tried to keep an eye on Kelton Fielding. A lot of these snowmobiles looked alike, and so did their riders. She was lucky Kelton was dressed a little more shabby than most of the other riders.

Kelton turned a corner to the right, and for a moment Swann panicked. "Oh come on!" she shouted as a snowmobile zipped past her on the right. How was she supposed to get over there? Another two sleds were approaching from behind on her right side. If she didn't turn now, she'd never make it.

Swann screamed as she cranked her handlebars, whipping

onto the side trail, losing speed as she bumped along a much rougher path. Sled after sled sped by on the main trail behind her. She kept going, struggling a little to keep moving through the deeper, fluffier snow. Kelton was well ahead of her now, around a bend in this first part of the shortcut. Swann laughed and hit the throttle to speed up. Her father would freak out when he saw her slide across that finish line. He'd be like, "Congratulations!" Then she'd take her helmet off and smile at him. His jaw would drop. She'd be a lot harder to ignore then.

She couldn't ignore the snowmobile ahead, rushing back toward her. She scrambled to squeeze the little brake handle in front of her left hand, but her glove caught for a moment. She screamed as the sled ahead of her flew up too close. The trail was too narrow for either of them to dodge the other. Finally she squeezed her brake handle with all her strength. Both snowmobiles came to a halt only two lengths apart.

Kelton's helmet was off a moment later. He did not look happy. "Who are—"

Swann slipped off her helmet and smiled.

"What are you doing here?" Kelton shouted. "Go back! You're off the trail!"

"Come on, Kelton," Swann said in her friendliest voice. "We're science partners. And you weren't going to tell me about your shortcut?" She was surprised at his instant transformation from openmouthed shock and disbelief to the tight jaw and gritted teeth of anger. Or was it hurt?

"I found this route. I thought of it. I've worked—" He shoved a gloved fist into his other gloved palm. "For months for this. Just because your rich daddy—"

"You can keep the prize snowmobile and the money when I win," Swann said. She thought it best to interrupt him before he said something he couldn't take back. Not that she wouldn't forgive him. She tried not to be vengeful like some of the girls at her old school. But if Kelton had continued on the tired old "rich girl" complaint and then said he'd never allow her to take the shortcut, the two of them would be stuck in an impasse that would be difficult to escape. "I'm in this for fun. You can keep the prizes."

"Won't matter, because I'm the one who will win this race," Kelton snapped.

"Then you better get going, or you'll lose your advantage," Swann pointed out. "You can either sit here trying to convince me not to take the shortcut, which is useless because I'm going no matter what you say. Or you can get moving before all the other racers already pass checkpoint two."

Kelton pressed his lips together and blew a frustrated huff out through his nose, which steamed in the cold like the angry snorting of a bull. "Up ahead is Stone Cold Gap. It's stupid-dangerous. If you're not going absolutely full throttle when you hit the jump, you won't make it. You'll crash. You should go back."

He held his helmet up above his head, pausing for a moment before slipping it on. "But I don't care what you do. For real." Kelton shoved on his helmet and hit the throttle in quick short bursts while he cranked his machine around to head back toward his shortcut.

SWANN WATCHED AS HE PUT ON REAL SPEED, STANDING up off his seat with his knees bent a little. Faster and faster he went, kicking up a white cloud around and behind him that hid the bottom of his snowmobile and almost made him look like he was flying above the snow.

But then, in the distance, Kelton's sled popped up a little hill, and he really was flying, a lighter stream of snow trailing in his wake like a contrail behind a jet plane. Had he made the landing? Was he OK? She couldn't see.

She didn't know many in McCall very well. She'd promised herself she'd learn more about people, trying to keep an open mind, at least until she had a better sense of the way things really were. It wasn't easy. First impressions were tough to beat, and this Kelton Fielding guy didn't seem like much of a winner. At least that's how all the other kids acted. Hard to say if the crowd was right or wrong. They treated her pretty weird too. But whether or not Kelton was weird, Swann certainly didn't want him hurt or, worse, dead, right here on the snowmobile trail.

A moment later, in the distance, up the slope on the far side of the stream, Kelton's snowmobile slid to a halt. Was he stopping for her, waiting to see whether or not she made the jump? So much for not caring what she did. It wasn't too late. She could turn around and go back right now. If she gave up on this shortcut, she'd never win, but she could still have fun driving the race.

But then what would be the point of renting the snowmobile and everything? And it was more than a matter of money. The rental hadn't been that expensive, after all. It all came down to five years ago, when she was seven and wanted to learn to play cello. Mom had explained carefully and endlessly that their family was blessed so that buying a cello and paying for lessons wasn't much of a problem. Many families didn't have that luxury. But, Mom had explained, money didn't buy success. That only came through hard work. Both she and Swann's father had to work very hard to succeed in a tough business. "And above all," Mom had said, "we must never give up."

Mom hadn't meant that about a crazy snowmobile jump or a shortcut in a silly small-town race. Swann revved the engine a little. She hadn't forgotten her mom's lesson, and despite wanting to quit a bunch of times, she still played cello. Swann might not be an expert snowmobile rider, but she was also determined to not be a fragile spoiled rich girl who gave up on everything the moment it became difficult.

Without further thinking, and before she could chicken out, Swann slammed on her helmet and gunned her sled's engine, racing ahead full throttle faster and faster toward the little hill that formed the jump over the gap. "Stupid, stupid, stupid," she muttered to herself. What if Kelton's snowmobile was just a better, faster machine? What if his run had messed up the snow somehow, making the jump impossible? What if she was doing this wrong? She really didn't know anything about snowmobiles. A drop of sweat rolled down her cheek. She concentrated on driving the machine straight down the path Kelton had taken. This was stupid, stupid, stupid.

The snowmobile sped along faster, faster, faster. The hill drew closer, closer, closer. Swann gripped the handlebars tightly, stood up like Kelton had done. The sled hit the hill. Swann screamed.

She was so high. Flying. She was going to die. The opposite bank approached fast. She kept screaming.

Her machine hit the ground, she flew forward, chest into the handlebars as she flopped back down on her seat. The sled jerked to the right. She cranked it left before she hit a tree, but overcompensated and almost rolled the thing. Finally she straightened out and hit the brake, sliding to a stop in the middle of the trail.

A long-held breath burst out of her, fogging up her helmet visor, so that she flipped it up. "Yes!" She screamed again, happier this time. "Woo! That was awesome!"

Kelton stood on his snowmobile about twenty yards away. He flashed her a thumbs-up before turning back around and speeding up the trail. Swann took a deep breath. She was still in the race.

SUPERPOP MADE THE JUMP. YEAH, HE HATED SWANN FOR trying to steal his shortcut. But even if she was a spoiled rich girl, there was no denying she had a certain spark of coolness just for having the guts to try the jump. And she'd made it! Plus, even if he did hate her, he wasn't a psycho who wanted her hurt or killed by coming up short on Stone Cold Gap.

But that was it. She was alive. OK. Good. Fine. Kelton cranked the throttle, heard his sled's motor rev higher, felt the speed and vibration though his body as he plowed ahead. She was crazy if she thought he would let her win. From now on, she was on her own. This would be the last he would see of her until after he was safely across the finish line.

After a few minutes, he'd cleared the creek valley, and the trail began to rise up the pass between the two peaks. This wasn't a maintained trail. The woods closed in on both sides, small supple branches slapping his arms, chest, and head like a hundred little whips, as though the mountain were trying to punish him, saying, *Go back!*

"Never!" Kelton shouted to the mountain. "You won't beat me." The snow was deep and he started weaving side to side a little to help the machine's track get a better bite and keep on pushing through. A thicker branch whapped his face, and not for the first time he was grateful for his helmet. He slapped his sled again. "Come on. You can do it."

Higher and higher up an increasingly steep slope Kelton and his snowmobile fought. After the trail cleared the thick tangle of shrubbery near the creek valley floor, the woods thinned out a little, but the snow was even deeper. Kelton risked a look back. Behind him, in the packed and broken trail he was forcing through the thick powder, SuperPop was having a much easier time.

But in the distance behind her, approaching fast, was another snowmobile. "Come on, man!" Someone else either knew about his shortcut, was taking a chance following him, or was determined to bring him back to the main race route. Well, tough luck. Kelton wouldn't allow either of those two to overtake him, and he darn sure wasn't going back to the main trail and last place in the race.

Kelton loved it, the roar, the high whine of his powerful snowmobile, the sound of his two pursuers back behind him. He ripped powder all the way up the first hill out of the valley. Too steep for a rail line, this must have been a horse-and-wagon road, or just a mule path. He would bet those old gold miners or whoever made the trail would have loved a machine like his.

But at the top of hill, he hit the brakes. "Oh no." The path ahead was completely gone. In the valley below was a mess of trees and branches, half buried in a deep and thick snow soup. His sled would be hopelessly stuck, buried in powder or snagged on a branch, within seconds.

It must have been an avalanche. They were so common, especially in backcountry snowmobiling, that the state of Idaho recommended and offered a free course about them. With all the snow they'd had through the last week, it wasn't surprising that the trail ahead had been blocked. Kelton had prepared for this. Well, he'd watched a ton of videos to try to prepare for this.

He'd have to go around the mess at the bottom of the valley ahead by side-hilling along one of the two side slopes. He'd practiced the tricky body position needed for the technique as well as he could on his stationary sled in the garage. Driving a snowmobile across the side of a mountain like that, preventing the sled from rolling or ghost-sledding out of control down that steep slope, required a lot of technique and concentration. The trouble was, side-hilling wasn't about speed. It was a slow, careful method.

The high whine of his two pursuers roared close as Swann and the other sledder slid up and stopped near him. Kelton pulled his helmet off. Swann did too.

Who else had followed him?

The other rider removed his helmet and Kelton wanted to punch him. "Hunter! Come on, man! What are you doing here?" Of course Richie Hunter Higgins, whose family had everything, including a zillion snowmobiles, was trying to steal the shortcut he, Kelton, had discovered.

"Yeah," Hunter said. "Swann saw your map. If you're going to cheat, you ought to be more careful about keeping your secrets."

Kelton glared at Swann. Of course the Richie SuperPop was doing all she could to ruin this for him. That's what Populars did. They thought it was fun to make Grits like him miserable.

"It's not cheating, Higgins," Kelton fired back. "There's nothing in the race rules says we gotta stay on the course. You might know that if you had done the work of figuring all this out like I did." He was wasting time. He could feel the race slipping away with every moment he delayed. "You two go back. The trail ahead isn't really passable. It's going to take some serious backcountry shredding to get over the pass."

"Serious backcountry . . ." Hunter circled his finger in front of his chest in a *blah-blah-blah* gesture. "You're acting like a snowmobile pro, when you just got that thing running like yesterday."

"Yeah, because I had to actually do the work. I didn't have it all handed to me by my daddy like you." Kelton wanted to destroy Hunter, but he hated fighting, and anything like that would take too long. "I'm going to win this race. I jumped Stone Cold Gap, no problem. I can do the rest." Hunter fidgeted and looked away for a moment. Kelton smiled. "You didn't make the jump, did you?"

"Only because that's stupid," Hunter fired back. "I'm not going to kill myself and wreck my snowmobile on a dumb jump when I can just go downstream to this place where I can ford the creek."

"Me and Swann made the jump," Kelton said. He exchanged a smile with Swann. "It's OK, dude. You just have to find some courage is all."

"There's courage, and there's stupidity," Hunter said.

"You guys!" Swann shouted. "There's a race?"

"Right," Kelton said. "Look, the trail ahead is blocked. I'm going to side-hill the right-hand slope to get around this, and then go back on the road where it rises up the next ascent. You two go back. Side-hilling is kind of tricky. If you try it and end up rolling down the mountain getting stuck, that's on you. I ain't your babysitter. Don't care what happens to you. For real."

Swann blipped her engine and then sang, "Whatever you can do, I can do it better."

"Yeah?" Kelton said. "Eat snow, SuperPop." He shoved on his helmet and hit his throttle, heading off to the right and giving the sled more power to scramble up the slope. Once again, he remembered the snowmobiling fundamentals video he'd watched at the library, and how the pro had reminded sledders to remember to breathe. It made a lot of sense now as he gritted his teeth and scurried up the steep side of the mountain.

When he was about two hundred feet up, he eased his sled to the left while hopping over his seat so that he stood with only his left foot canted forty degrees on the right running board. His heart slammed for a second as the snowmobile began to roll left down the mountain, but Kelton quickly counter-steered, just like he'd seen in the video. "Square your shoulders to direction of travel," he said, talking himself through the steps. "Then just blip the throttle for a little speed. Brake. Blip it. Counter-steer." There was no trail, but he had to keep the sled level, or else he and his machine were going rolling. So on he went, slow and steady, with just his sled's track and the back of its right ski on the slope, the left ski mostly out of the snow. Kelton held the handlebars, stood with his left foot on the right running board, and kept most of his body out to the right of the sled, sort of walking it along with his right foot stepping in the snow after every blip. It wasn't the quickest mode of travel, but it would be faster than fighting through the mess in the basin down below.

"Oh no, no, no!" The front of his sled's right ski caught the snow, and threatened to slap the rest of his snowmobile flat on the steep slope. He'd roll in seconds. Kelton counter-steered and regained control. His hands ached with tension on the handlebars as he struggled along, blip-brake-step, blip-brake-step.

It was working. He was doing it. But it wasn't easy. The whole way across the slope, he felt the pull of the sled as it wanted to lie flat on its track and both skis, and for the entire way he had to fight against that pull, counter-steering and giving the sled just enough speed to keep going.

Finally he'd cleared the cluttered low basin, steered back to the trail, and begun his ascent again. Ahead, the trail wound up to its highest elevation between the two peaks before it would start down the other side. There would be another sort of bowl on the other side with the valley descending to a small lake before winding back down to the main race trail.

Kelton checked on his unwanted company. They were three-quarters of the way across the basin behind and below him. Stuck. It looked like one of them had tried to side-hill it, but had ended up sliding and tumbling down the hill. It must have been Swann. She was the braver of the two. He felt a flash of guilt, but then reminded himself he'd tried to warn them both to go back. Plus neither looked hurt.

Hunter kicked at his sled and flapped his arms around before yanking on the handlebars. Kelton laughed. Finally Mr. Popular was getting what he deserved. And if he didn't know how to get his sled unstuck, then he definitely shouldn't have come out here in the first place. He'd have to fend for himself.

Swann had managed to rock her snowmobile free and was advancing through the basin almost to the bottom of the trail slope below Kelton. He couldn't deny it. That girl was tough. "Yeah," Kelton said out loud. "But she can't beat me."

Kelton put the throttle on and continued his ascent. The first part of it was relatively easy going, but the farther he went, the steeper the slope became. Tons of snow down around McCall meant even more snow at elevation. Now those first few flakes falling at the start of the race had been joined by more of their friends, the beginning of what might become a new storm. Higher elevation, more snow, steeper slope. These were all prime conditions for an avalanche.

Still, he was almost halfway up this final push to the top. Once he was over the divide, it would be a lot easier coming down. If he hurried, he could still make it, maybe still win this race, even if the delays caused by the other two had slowed him down. It would be a lot closer than he expected, but victory was still possible.

About three-quarters of the way up, the ground leveled out a little, the snow so deep he was shredding powder among the tops of small pine trees. Behind him, the view stretched on beyond the basin all the way to Stone Cold Gap, and the main trail a good run past that.

The snowfall had picked up, and the wind. And Kelton wasn't sure if it was his imagination or if the snow caked on his pathetic gear was starting to chill through to his body. He clapped his hands against the cold tingle in his fingers, and stomped his running boards, trying to warm his feet.

Swann was still pursuing, and Hunter, in distant third among them, had finally freed his sled and resumed the chase, at last reaching the slope out of the basin and starting to work his way up.

"Time to get going again," Kelton said. The snow was falling in faster, bigger flakes, especially way up above the path he'd just taken up the eastern slope. Kelton took in a sharp breath and yanked off his helmet, blinking and watching the east mountain again. It wasn't just a snowstorm! Above a massive outcropping of rock up there, snow plumes burst in all directions like the white-hot core of big fireworks in the sky on the Fourth of July. Then the rocks were gone, erased by a growing cascade of snow, like a bubbling, expanding mist.

"Avalanche!" Kelton screamed down to the others. "Get out of there!"

Swann must have seen the problem. She started veering to the left as she made the climb toward Kelton. Good. If she could reach a higher elevation she could get above the rushing snowslide. But Hunter? He was way down there, and the giant wave of snow was coming fast.

He'd told them to go back. Why hadn't they just turned around and gone back? Kelton bit his lip and watched helplessly as, in seconds, both Swann and Hunter vanished in a rushing white cloud. Kelton looked down on an angry swirling blankness below him, down in the basin where two of his classmates used to be.

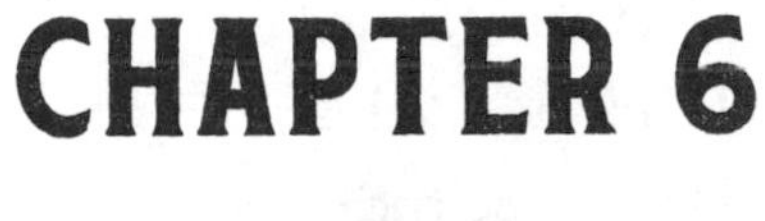

CHAPTER 6

SWANN SCREAMED AS SNOW SWIRLED ANGRILY IN THE AIR all around her, an instant blizzard-like whiteout. Despite the sheer whiteness of it all, the landscape around her grew dark, and she couldn't see farther than a few feet. She had no idea where she was going, no way to know if she was about to strike a boulder or a tree. Desperate, she drove her snowmobile uphill. Or at least in the direction she thought was uphill. Instantly her whole body, arms, legs, chest, and her entire snowmobile were covered in a thick layer of snow.

Was she going to be buried? Was she going to die out here? Her body shook, and her snowmobile's engine screamed in its high-pitched whine as she helplessly squeezed her handlebars, full throttle blindly ahead.

Her left hand slipped off the handle as her snowmobile hit something and rocked dangerously to one side, but she righted it and kept going.

The area around her began to brighten. She could see farther ahead, first a tree up the slope in the distance, then a blip of something red, and a person higher up the hill.

"Kelton!" she yelled. But of course he couldn't hear her until she finally pulled up onto his plateau. There she stopped, killed her engine, and slid off her sled, slapping her arms and chest to find her own body inside the snowman. Then she took off her helmet, the biting cold wind a welcome reminder she was still alive.

"You OK?" Kelton asked. But he was preoccupied, staring back down into the chaos below, pacing. He looked up into the rapidly falling snow, pressing his hands over his face. "No. No, no, no. I told him to go back. I told him."

Swann stepped closer to him, reaching out to touch his shoulder but stopping herself. "Kelton?"

"You're OK?" he asked again, finally looking at her.

"Yeah," she said, as much to assure herself as him. "I'm fine. It was just, like, snowing super-hard down there." She looked down the mountain too. "Hunter?"

Kelton said nothing, but stood there, staring. Finally he shook his head. "We gotta get down there. Find him. If he's buried, we won't have long."

He started back toward his snowmobile, but Swann grabbed his arm. Was it her imagination, or did she hear something besides the wind? Maybe she was just remembering the constant buzz-roar of her own snowmobile. But the sound was louder, changing pitch. "Kelton!"

Kelton rushed to her side. "No way!" He smiled, laughed a little. "Come on, man," he said quietly.

Soon the noise was unmistakable. A snowmobile engine's low roar punctuated by higher-pitched throttled-up whines.

At last Hunter materialized out of the cloud, and hurried to their position, like Swann had been, completely plastered in a layer of snow. He looked like a marble statue, or someone trapped within a statue, beginning to crack out, as the snow fell away from him.

Hunter took off his helmet. "Woo! Oh, that was close!"

Swann laughed. The situation had changed so fast, from dangerous and terrifying, to fearful and sad, to relieved and therefore kind of hilarious. "We thought you were buried."

Hunter bent over with his hands on his knees, letting out a big breath. "No, I don't think the snow actually shifted around me, just fallout from the tumbling snowpack up on the mountain. But it was like a snowstorm coming at me from every direction at the same time. I could barely see."

Swann gave him a little punch in the shoulder. It would have been hard for her to explain it, but she felt like she and Hunter were closer, not in a boyfriend-girlfriend way, but as though they were in some kind of club, the almost-trapped-in-an-avalanche society of the Idaho backcountry. "Yeah, I know! That was intense. Like it turned into night in one second." The more she talked about it, the more the fear and shakiness fell away.

Hunter slapped her high-five, their gloved hands clapping

with a thick hollow sound. It was one of the first genuine celebrations she'd had with anyone from McCall. Plenty of people wanted to hang out with her to talk about Hollywood or to see if they could get a *Snowtastrophe* action figure autographed by her dad or something. Nobody ever seemed to want to know or connect with her. Not really. But this was something new. It was hard to be more real than this.

"It should be safe now," Kelton said. "Safer, anyway. I mean, the mountain can't have avalanches all day. Eventually the snow settles down. Let's head back."

"What?" Hunter shouted. "Who's the chicken now, Fielding?"

Oh no. Swann rolled her eyes. Here they went, typical guys doing typical macho one-up bragging and put-downs.

"You two could have been killed," Kelton said. "And there's only going to be a greater risk of avalanche the higher we go, especially when it's snowing heavy like this."

"We got through that just fine," Hunter said. "You talk so big and bad about being brave enough to jump Stone Cold Gap, but then you're afraid of getting a little snow on you?"

"An avalanche can put more than a little snow on us, Hunter. I'm serious."

"I'm serious," Swann said. "Serious about winning this race, and all this arguing is seriously dumb. See you at the finish line, suckers!"

"Swann, the chances of winning the race now are so slim," Kelton began.

Swann laughed, slipped her helmet back on, and ran as best she could in the deep snow. Then she was back on her snowmobile, yanking the cable to start the engine. They were through the worst of it. If she hurried up, she could make it over the pass and back down to the racecourse in time to be right there with the leaders. If she played it right, this avalanche thing could work out in her favor, allowing her to get ahead of both Kelton and Hunter.

Swann cranked the throttle hard to get her snowmobile moving in the deep snow, and then sped farther up the trail.

"SWANN, NO!" KELTON SHOUTED. HE EXCHANGED A worried look with Hunter. Well, he, Kelton, was worried. Hunter had this snide look on his face, the expression that so many of the Populars saved for him, that kind of sneer that was a mix between pity and hate, like Kelton wasn't good enough for any of them. Hunter ran for his sled. Kelton ran faster, or basically hobbled in the deep snow, for his own. They were typical Pops, thinking they were always right, trying to hog all the credit for themselves. He'd started his snowmobile and was speeding off after Swann, only about four sled lengths behind her. Hunter soon pursued Kelton at about the same distance.

Kelton blipped the throttle as he bumped up over a big snow mound, jumping through the air for a moment, standing with his body centered in good position to easily stick the landing and continue after Swann. She slowed down for a moment in a deep powder trap and suddenly Kelton was right beside her.

If these two wanted to be cutthroat about this, they should have prepared better. This was stupid. They weren't even halfway through his shortcut and already they'd been dangerously close to an avalanche. Where they were heading, they were bound to run into more problems. But even if it was next to impossible for him to win the whole race, he wasn't going to let spoiled Hunter and rich SuperPop beat him. No way.

They didn't ride well. Swann stayed in her seat most of the time, and Hunter was all over the place, leaning the wrong way. They both rode with their center of balance way off, inviting the chance to be thrown off or to dump their sleds over sideways. The way they rode, they could end up stuck out here all through the nasty cold night.

It took a while, but eventually Kelton passed Swann. Thing was, cool though she might have been, it felt good to pull ahead of her in an open race. He shredded powder all the way up to the summit of the pass. He would not stop. Those two clowns were on their own. He didn't care what happened to them. For real.

The wind blew fiercely at the top of the pass. Kelton could feel it whipping at his coat, and he had to keep wiping the snow off his helmet's visor. The cold was beginning to bite through his clothing now. Snow had worked its way between the gap in his sleeves and gloves, between his pants and coat. Worse than just cold, now he was wet. A terrible combination, and possibly dangerous. If he'd had a real snowmobile suit, decent boots, and the right kind of gloves, he'd probably be fine. But the world never did Kelton Fielding any favors. He'd have to push through with what he had.

"All downhill from here," he said as he sped ahead, faster now, heading down the slope. He jumped his sled right off a four-foot drop, landing like a pro, remaining standing with his body square and his knees bent a little, so he could maintain control while absorbing the impact. Then he jumped another, slightly smaller drop.

The other two were moving slower, maybe trying to figure out a seemingly safer way down the mountain. Kelton laughed as he zipped on ahead. Hunter acted brave and tough, but when it came to a rougher trail like this, he had nothing. Swann was braver than Hunter, but lacked Kelton's skill. In only a few minutes Kelton had stretched out his lead to a distance of about two football fields.

This was good, because the trail ahead looked even more blocked than the route through the basin on the way up. Despite having to drive slowly, he'd make better time side-hilling it than through the very deep powder and the rest of the mess of very dense woods in the bottom of the valley. One thing his map didn't prepare him for was the possibility that the road, even though it was on the map, wasn't much of a road anymore, and had become quite overgrown. The trees were thinner up on the left slope. It was a little trickier side-hilling on the left side, but he took it relatively slowly, riding the brake to keep control. Again he settled into a pattern: blip, brake, step. Blip, brake, step.

A serious chunk of rock protruded from the snow ahead of him, dropping in a ragged cliff clear to the valley floor. He'd have to go over it. Carefully, he eased the front of his sled more toward the top of the mountain, giving it plenty of power, to fight his way up the steep slope. He smiled. His snowmobile was a beast, its track biting hard and scrambling up that mountain until he'd risen above the level of the rock obstacle. Then he was back to the steady side-hill move.

When he'd cleared the rock, he figured he'd ease himself back down. It didn't make sense and wasn't the safest to ride this high. Besides, the trail looked clearer ahead, and it would be fastest to ride ahead down on the floor of the valley.

His sled lurched a little, kind of a side slide that made his heart leap. He thought his snowmobile was rolling flat on the steep slope. That would lead to an uncontrolled tumble down the mountain. Then he heard the *whumph* sound, even over the engine noise and through his helmet. Above him a crack shot through the smooth surface of the snow, jagged like lightning. Another crack below him.

Kelton drew in a deep breath. He tried to speed up, tried to get away. "No, no, please," he whined. This couldn't be happening. Not when he was right in the middle of it. About thirty feet up the mountain, the snow seemed to explode. It was as if all that white had come alive, was furious with Kelton and rocketing at him, sliding away all around him. It rumbled, and his snowmobile turned all over out of control as the whole mountain seemed to shift. Kelton was caught in the middle of a massive avalanche.

He throttled up, trying to outrun the worst of it, but the snow slid right out from under his track and the sled was hard to control. Then a wall of white slammed his body and he flew off his snowmobile.

He screamed, hit the ground, tumbled. Dark, light, dark. Snow flew in all around him. Not like being in a blizzard, but like heavy powder clamping onto his body from all sides. The avalanche videos he'd watched told him to keep trying to swim, to chop his arms like doing a crawl stroke on the lake, in order to stay above the snow.

But he tumbled. It was impossible. He couldn't even tell which way was up. Kelton screamed until he remembered something else from the video. He drew a deep breath, doing all he could to expand his body, his only chance of preventing his chest from being compressed by the snow, his only chance of being able to move or breathe the slightest bit.

And then it was dark. Very dark, and very cold.

MIKE IRONS SIPPED STRONG BLACK COFFEE FROM A battered old thermos as he sat on his snowmobile. A large bear of a man, he ran his fingers through his beard and then shook his papers. All racers had passed checkpoint two. All racers except for three twelve-year-olds. A kid named Kelton Fielding, a girl—the daughter of the rich actor who'd donated the prize snowmobile—Swann Siddiq, and Mike's own nephew, his brother-in-law's son, Hunter Higgins.

"Maybe they're just messing around," said the other checkpoint two volunteer, Allie Hennes, a certified paramedic and also a member of the McCall Area Snowmobile Club. "You know, kind of giving up on the race, zigzagging around. Snowball fights, maybe."

"Yeah, maybe," Mike said. "You're probably right." Still, something about this bothered him. He knew snowmobiles, and he knew this course. Even playing around, stopping once in a while to look at the scenery, those kids should have been coming into range by now.

"Or mechanical trouble," Allie said quietly.

"Let's hope." Mike pulled out his radio and pressed the transmit button. "Checkpoint one, this is checkpoint two, over." He released the transmit button so he could receive. After a long moment he keyed to transmit again. "Checkpoint one, come in, over."

Finally the low static on the radio went quiet while someone else transmitted.

Two, this is one. Go ahead, over.

Mike couldn't remember the name of the guy on checkpoint one. This was the guy's first year volunteering to help with the race. "What is your location?"

Checkpoint one. All packed up. Just about to head back to town.

It's mighty cold out here, and getting colder. Weatherman says this storm blowing in could be a lot of snow. We plan to be warm in the bar by the time it gets too bad.

Mike whipped the radio around in an impatient circle, waiting for the guy to stop yapping. When he finally shut up about the bar, Mike radioed back, "Checkpoint one. Have a look at your list. Verify you've accounted for all racers."

Oooookaaay, the man radioed back. *Stand by.*

Allie shot Mike a worried look. Mike tugged his beard. The checkpoint one guy was taking forever.

Checkpoint two, this is checkpoint one. I've looked our list over twice just now. Every racer who entered the race has cleared this checkpoint. Is there a problem?

Mike radioed back. "Could be. Stay on your station for now. The bar will have to wait. Checkpoint two, out."

Had he somehow missed three racers passing through his checkpoint? All kids? What were the odds? He radioed to checkpoint three asking if his missing racers had come through, but not everyone had passed the third checkpoint yet.

He put the radio back in the pouch on his coat. "Allie, you get on your sled and you fly to checkpoint three. Keep an eye out along the way. You got the sled numbers of those kids from the list. Then check with the people at three. Maybe . . ." Mike shook his head. "Maybe the kids slipped by us in the crowd and we somehow didn't get them checked in."

"Yeah," Allie said with a doubtful look. "Good luck." She

slammed on her helmet, jumped on her sled, pull-started it up, and sped off down the race trail. In the increasingly heavy snowfall, she faded quickly into the white.

Mike tugged his beard again, then pulled out his cell phone. Coverage out here was spotty at best. He tried calling the sheriff's office. No luck. He and Sheriff Hank were old fishing buddies, so he tried calling the sheriff's personal cell phone directly. Nothing.

He swapped out his cell phone for his radio. "Checkpoint one, this is Mike Irons, about to leave checkpoint two. You're closer to town. Call Sheriff Hamlin. Tell him we might have a problem. He needs to meet me at your location ASAP. You stay there. I'm on my way to your position."

Mike put the radio in his pocket, slipped his helmet on, fired up his sled, and took off best speed back along the racecourse. Yeah, this could be nothing. But Mike Irons hadn't been snowmobiling this long without developing a certain sense for trouble. The weather was steadily worsening and this didn't feel right. He was going to do all he could to make sure his nephew and those other kids were safe.

CHAPTER 7

"KELTON!" SWANN SCREAMED HOPELESSLY. THERE WAS NO way he could hear her through her helmet, over the noise of her snowmobile, and in that massive frozen cascade ahead of her. She stopped, to avoid driving right into it, and she watched Kelton struggle to drive out of danger. One moment he was on his snowmobile and in the next second both were gone, as though the snow had erased them from existence. She thought she saw him once after that, a flash of darker color in the middle of that blast of snow, but then all was white. "Kelton, no!"

It seemed to take a long time for the snow to finally settle, and once it had, Swann kept her eyes on the last place she'd seen a sign of him. Then she cranked up her throttle and sped toward that location as fast as she could. The valley was an even worse mess now than it had been before, a battle to move through. And when she finally reached the area where the snow had settled, she wasn't sure at all where to begin looking.

Could he have survived being caught in the middle of that avalanche? If he was still alive, could he breathe under the snow?

No way. It had to be impossible. How deep would he be? Where should she start digging? Even if she found the right place to dig, could she get him out before he suffocated down there?

Hunter slid up on his snowmobile, killed his engine, and scrambled to join her. "Oh no. Is he somewhere in this?"

"Yeah," Swann pulled her helmet off. "I saw it all. It just clobbered him."

"What do we do?" Hunter removed his helmet.

"Just start digging," Swann had no idea what to do, but she knew they couldn't wait around talking about it. She pointed to a certain spot on the slope. "Um, I'm guessing he has to be below that point. So let's work kind of in a line, punch down into the snow the best you can. We'll try to feel for him first. If you feel something solid down there, start digging. See what it is."

Hunter nodded, and the two of them high-stepped through the deep snow to the place she'd indicated. She refused to check her watch and tried not to think about how long Kelton had been under. They punched the snow, trying to reach down to find something. But she couldn't get her hand super-deep. If he was too low, she'd miss him.

Then he'd die down there.

"Kelton, can you hear me?" Hunter called out.

Swann frowned. "Do you think—"

"I don't know if he can hear down there. If he's even . . . I mean, I've never been buried like this. So I don't—"

"Kelton!" Swann yelled. "Kelton, we're coming for you. Hang in there."

"Hey!" Hunter called out with such enthusiasm Swann looked up from where she was searching. "Look! Blaze-orange! The flag from his sled, maybe!"

"If it's still attached to his snowmobile. If he is still with his snowmobile," Swann said. "You go check it out. I'll keep searching."

They dug around and called for Kelton for what seemed like forever.

"Where is he?" Hunter shouted, digging with fury around the orange flag. Digging down, down. "Kelton, come on, try to answer me. Scream and maybe I'll hear you and find you."

The two of them kept digging. It was all taking far too long.

"Here's the sled!" Hunter called out. He dug with greater speed and fury, grunting, rushing to move the snow. "Where is he? Where is he? He's not here!"

Swann bit her lip. This was terrible. Kelton had wanted to go back. He'd warned about the danger of going ahead, and now he was gone. This was her fault. She might have basically killed him.

DARKNESS. COLD. WAS HE ALIVE? KELTON WIGGLED HIS toes in his boots. He groaned within his helmet. "Of course you're alive," he said to himself. "Otherwise how could you be cold?" Then he remembered that talking used up oxygen. He tried to kick, but his legs wouldn't move. His arms were held fast too, his right arm stretched way back, kind of above his head, like he was raising his hand in class.

Why couldn't he move? Was he paralyzed? Had he broken his back? Was that why he couldn't move? Maybe that was stupid. If he'd broken his back, why did nothing hurt? But that's what paralysis was, right? Something gets broken and you can't feel anything.

He groaned, fought to move. "No, please," he whimpered.

You can wiggle your toes in your boots. You can wiggle your fingers. You're not paralyzed. You're stuck in the snow. Working through the ideas in his mind helped him calm down, slow his breathing and the use of oxygen. How much useful air could there be inside the little space within his helmet? Not much. And no way air could get through all this snow.

Kelton Fielding had a few minutes left to live.

It was so cold. The snow, where it had blasted up his shirt on his back, where it had pushed down the tops of his boots, where it had slid up his sleeves and into his gloves, hurt so bad. It was absolutely freezing, but felt like it was burning his flesh, or cutting him, eating him. More than anything, he wanted to move to wipe the searing cold snow off his skin.

Maybe he'd die of the cold before he ran out of air.

What would it feel like to die of suffocation? Would it be like holding his breath underwater? That tightness in the chest, pounding in the head, fingers tingling, urgent desperation to burst with a gasp. Or would he simply get quiet and tired, maybe a little confused as the last of the air ran out?

His eyes stung. Would he use up air faster if he cried? Would they laugh at him when they found his body with tears frozen around his eyes and on his cheeks?

They'd notify his mom. The police would come to the house and she'd think he'd done something bad until the cop told her he was missing. By the time he told her that, Kelton would be long dead. Would she even miss him?

He sobbed. Would anyone miss him? Mom wouldn't have to work extra shifts to buy him shoes or whatever. Wouldn't have to worry about fixing him supper. Wouldn't be angry about another bad report card.

He doubted anyone at school would miss him. Maybe Milo Tanner would say it was a shame he was gone. But the teachers wouldn't have to lecture him about his grades anymore. Ms. Foudy wouldn't be mad at him for talking during study time again. Hunter Higgins wouldn't have to put up with his questions.

Hunter. And Swann. How big had the avalanche been? Were they buried alive, freezing and slowly suffocating in the dark right now like he was? They'd die too. Hunter's family would be crushed. The whole school would shut down for the funeral. Swann's death would be all over the news. Fancy Hollywood types would tweet about how sad it was. The articles would talk about the death of the daughter of the actor and actress, along with the son of the important local lawyer, and . . . and the other kid.

Thing was, Hunter wasn't such a bad guy if Kelton really

thought about it. He was patient when Kelton kept talking to him during study time. Hunter hadn't ever made fun of him like Bryden or some of the other guys.

And Swann. Wow. Swann Siddiq. Even her name sounded like a song. And she looked like . . . an angel. With that completely black hair, and her dark eyes, that bright smile. And the girl had guts too. She hit that jump with no hesitation. Sure, she was rich. An off-the-charts SuperPop. But when she had been assigned to work with him in science yesterday, she hadn't acted all superior or like working with him was super-terrible, the way McKenzie or Morgan might have done. Swann was either a great actress hiding her hate for him well, or she was kind of cool.

Now Kelton had led both Swann and Hunter out here to their deaths.

And who would feed Scruffy now? Would that little fuzzball be shivering out in the cold on his chain in his dirt spot, wondering why Kelton never brought him anything to eat anymore?

Kelton sobbed. "Sorry, little pup," he whispered as he shivered. He was so sorry for so many things.

"THERE'S NO RECEPTION OUT HERE!" HUNTER SHOUTED. "That thing is useless! Help me dig!"

Hunter was right. Not one bar. Swann slipped her phone in her pocket and threw herself back into digging.

"He's not down here!" Hunter shouted. "I've got the snowmobile, but he's not here!"

Swann wiped her eyes. "We gotta keep looking. Look somewhere else. We have to look, like, everywhere." She cursed. "How long has he been . . . How long's it been?" She kept fighting through the deep snow, stopping every foot or so to reach down as deep as she could.

"I don't know." Hunter climbed out of the pit he'd dug around the snowmobile. He began scrambling like Swann. "He's been under about two minutes. Maybe three."

Swann shot Hunter a nervous glance. "How long can—"

"No idea." Hunter crawled across the snow, trying to dig down with his legs and arms. "Keep looking. Kelton! Can you hear me? Try to shout!"

Swann could hold her breath for about a minute and a half, maybe a little longer if she was absolutely forced to do so. Three minutes? No way. More and more, she felt like they were searching, not for a guy from their class, but for a dead body.

She was breathing hard, heart pounding. Pushing through this deep snow required a lot of work. Was she slowing down? Was Hunter? Why? Because they were tired? Or because it was less and less likely that hurrying actually mattered?

"No," she groaned through gritted teeth. She would not slow down, could not give up. She forced herself to take two more big steps. Her steps were too big, it turned out, because she lost her balance and fell over on her side, reaching out instinctively to break her fall, but of course her arm pushed right into the snow. And her fingers hit something solid that moved a little.

"What?" She slid closer to whatever was down there and started shoving snow away. "Hey, Hunter?" she said. She brushed away snow and found the black tips of a glove. She squeezed them. Fingers inside! The fingers wiggled. "Hunter!" Her scream echoed through the whole valley. "Found him! He's alive! Get over here! Help me!"

Swann Siddiq ceased to exist. There were only her hands shoving away snow, moving in a blur, clawing at the white. "Kelton, we're coming! Kelton, hang in there! Kelton, can you hear me?"

Hunter slid right into her and scrambled to push the snow away too. "Are we on top of him? Maybe we're crushing him."

"Just dig! The snow is crushing him." She cursed savagely. "I'd give anything for a shovel right now."

Finally a whole black-gloved hand was above the snow. It moved, all fingers but the thumb bending just a little, as though Kelton were trying to give a thumbs-up gesture, but was frozen stiff. Swann and Hunter punched and pulled and clawed. Her cold fingertips ached from ripping at the snow. Maybe they were bleeding. She didn't care. Soon his arm was dug out. "Where's his head? We have to clear an airway."

Her fingers hit something hard. "Helmet!" Seconds later the round black dome of the top of his helmet was cleared.

"Swann," said Hunter. "What if his neck is broken? Fractured or something? If we move his head too much we might do more harm than good."

"None of that will matter if he can't breathe." The frantic digging had reduced Swann to a savage beast. She panted, grunted, and dug like mad, loosening and pushing away the more packed-in snow. Hunter pulled the extra snow out of the growing pit so it wouldn't slide back down on top of Kelton.

"Hey." Her fingers slid down the front of his helmet and gripped his visor. "I'm going to pull this up, get some air in there."

"Won't a bunch of snow fall right in?" Hunter asked. "He has to be cold enough al—"

She flipped up his visor. "Kelton! Can you hear me?" Some snow crumbles rolled into his helmet. She clapped her hands, trying to shake snow off her gloves before fingering around in there trying to pull snow out. Still there was no answer. "Kelton! Kelton, please. Please answer me."

"So d-did you get a video of that?" Kelton asked quietly. "M-make a viral p-post?"

"No!" Swann shouted, laughing with relief. "Nobody cares about videos and social media at a time like this. I'm just glad you're alive."

"Oh. Well then, c-could you two please hurry up?" Kelton's voice sounded like someone talking through a long cardboard tube. "It's getting . . . kind of cold down here." Kelton sort of laughed, but his laughter, like his speech, was flat, squeezed so that he sounded like an out-of-breath runner trying to talk after a long hard race. He must have been packed in pretty tight down there. "Plus we're gonna really need to hurry . . . if we wanna . . . win the race."

Hunter and Swann laughed. Swann blinked several times. "Don't you worry, guy. Just breathe deep. We'll have you out of there fast."

"Yeah," Hunter said. "Just lie there. Take it easy."

"Oh, if I wasn't frozen, and . . . you know . . . buried in the snow . . ." Kelton chuckle-wheezed. "Swear I'd punch you for that."

CHAPTER 8

BY THE TIME MIKE IRONS REACHED CHECKPOINT ONE HE hadn't spotted a single sled the whole way back. He dismounted even before his own sled had come to a full stop and tugged his beard, looking around the area in the diminishing light and the increasing snowfall. The volunteer had been sitting sideways on his own snowmobile like it was a bench. He checked his watched as he stood up.

"Is there a problem?" the guy said. He was a kid. Couldn't be over twenty-five, and not too sharp, judging by the way he'd acted so far.

"Yeah," Mike said. "Pretty sure we got three missing kids, maybe lost out there in the snow."

A big SUV pulled into the parking lot down the little slope just off the trail. Mike jogged down there. The kid followed.

Sheriff Hank Hamlin stepped out, bundled up in boots, overalls, coat, and full equipment belt. "Mike," said the sheriff. He nodded at the kid. "Dylan. What's the trouble? We got missing racers?"

"Sorry to bother you, Sheriff," Dylan said. "Probably nothing. But—"

"Missing three kids. Daughter of that famous actor. My nephew Hunter Higgins. And that Fielding boy."

"Josie Abbott's son?" the sheriff asked.

"Think so," said Mike.

A sharp cutting wind whistled through the open parking lot and Sheriff Hank shivered. "You two been out here a long time. We could talk about this in the truck. Warm up a little?"

Dylan looked like he was willing, but Mike shook his head. "Thanks"—he gestured at the increasingly dark and snowy woods—"but we need to hurry. Especially if someone's hurt."

"We start searching?" Dylan said.

Sheriff Hank nodded. "I'll call the McCall police, ask them to check the kids' homes and to look around in town just in case the kids gave up on the race and went back."

Dylan checked his watch again. "The race ought to be about over by now. Maybe the last of the racers finishing up. The girl's father will probably be near the finish line to award the prize."

"Now, we don't want all those snowmobilers to help with the search," Mike said. "We'll just end up with more people missing. But we need our best local guys to start looking right away. If the kids went off-trail between checkpoints one and two . . . Well, that's a lot of ground to cover."

"Should I head for the finish line, to gather our best guys for the search?" Dylan offered.

Was this guy crazy? Mike shook his head. "No. You and

me are going to start searching off-trail starting from the first checkpoint." Mike looked up. The evening was turning miserable-snowy. "Snow coming down this hard is going to make it difficult to spot their tracks. First we'll comb the race trail, try to see if we can find a spot they turned off." He looked at the sheriff. "I sent Allie Hennes onward to the next checkpoint. Get in touch with her. Maybe we'll get lucky and she's found them."

"Let's hope so. I'll drive around to the finish line, check if the kids are there," said Sheriff Hank. "There's still a chance that this is a clerical error and they slipped past your checkpoint unnoticed."

Mike cursed. "I hope that's what happened."

"I can also notify the girl's folks and, like you said, get the best locals looking." The sheriff opened his truck door.

"Don't let 'em get too crazy, Hank," Mike said. "This is turning into a bad night. We send everybody off into the woods helter-skelter, we'll just make things worse."

"Lived all my life right here in the heart of Payette National Forest. Twenty-two years in law enforcement." Hank slapped Mike's arm. "This ain't my first search. I know it's not my nephew out there, but around here, our kids are our kids. We'll find 'em. Promise."

KELTON WAS USELESS. EVEN WHEN THEY HAD HIM DUG out down to his waist and he should have helped, he found he couldn't. His arms and fingers, his legs, were super-stiff. And when they finally pulled him all the way out of his snowy tomb, his legs below the knees didn't feel real. It was as though he were perched atop wobbly stilts. Kelton fought hard to push away paralysis fears.

He flopped down on his belly on top of the snow. "OK, so I can hardly feel my feet. That's not how paralysis works right? If you break your back, you lose all the legs, right? You lose control of your whole body below the point where you break your back, right?"

"Oh yeah," Hunter said. "You were just kind of walking."

"You're cold," Swann said. "Numb with cold."

"Like your hands get if you're having a snowball fight without gloves," Hunter added.

Kelton rolled over on his back. The snow was coming down even heavier than before, and it was getting dark. They didn't have much daylight left. "I gotta get back on my sled. We have to get out of here."

"Kelton, you almost died," Swann pointed out. "Maybe the race isn't so important?"

Kelton kicked his legs, trying to thaw them. It was the snow all down his boots that was his biggest problem. "No, forget the race." It hurt to say it, to give in to yet another failure in his life, but no matter what his teachers or anyone else thought, he was no dummy. "We're about out of daylight. It's only going to get colder. The snow is falling even heavier. It will be a lot harder to find our way back. An avalanche at night? Ain't nobody digging anybody out of that."

"There are headlights on our sleds," Hunter pointed out.

"Yeah, but they won't be much help, especially in this snowstorm," Kelton said. He was impressed that Hunter seemed to be taking what he said seriously.

"It's getting worse," Swann pointed out. "Like, a lot worse. I know I'm from California and may be a bad judge of snowstorms, but this is really coming down and blowing hard. Bigger than most of the snowstorms I've seen here."

Kelton grunted in cold, pain, and frustration. "I won't be able to drive my sled. I gotta warm up and thaw out. I have some dry clothes in my emergency pack. We need a fire."

"In this snow?" Swann asked. "Is that possible?"

"The snowmobile pro guy on the YouTube video did it."

Swann laughed. "Well, good. That's all we need."

"There's the mine," Hunter suggested. "Up on the hill behind us. Back there a couple hundred yards."

Swann frowned. "What do you mean, a mine? Like a gold mine? A coal mine?"

Kelton bit his lip and groaned as he forced himself to his feet. "Abandoned gold mine. It's why this road is here." It hurt to shrug. "Well, there's sort of a road here. Swann, they call Idaho the gem state for a reason. Still, every kid who grows up in Idaho is told a zillion times that abandoned mines are dangerous."

"Can't be more dangerous than freezing to death," Hunter said. "If you have to be warmed up before we go home, the mine is your best chance."

Kelton groaned again, forcing himself to move to his sled.

"Right. We go to the mine. Just hope my snowmobile is up to it. So you g-guys thought I w-was buried with my snowmobile? Wish I had been. Got out sooner."

"How could it still run?" Swann asked. "After it was so far under. The only part of it above the snow was the tip of the orange flag."

"W-well," said Kelton, "it is d-designed to run in the snow. I mean . . . that's its whole point." Kelton groaned in pain, gritting his teeth, as he forced his fingers to curl around the handle of the pull start.

Hunter moved toward him. "Here, let me do it."

"I got it!" Kelton shouted. "You two get your snowmobiles started. " He grunted as he finally forced his hand into a firm hold on the handle. "Come on, snowmobile. I need you. Let's . . ." He yanked the pull start. The engine coughed and then roared. "Fire up! Yeah!"

"Woo-hoo!" Swann shouted. "First try!"

Kelton flopped down on the seat. He wouldn't be able to stand and ride his snowmobile like the pros. He'd have to hang himself over the handlebars and steer with his whole upper torso, his hands being the frozen useless clumps they were. "Hunter! You saw the place. You lead the way."

Hunter grabbed the pull start on his own sled. Then he stopped and looked back at Kelton. "You sure you're up to this? I mean, you were just completely buried in—"

"It's really c-cold out here," Kelton said sharply.

"Let's go, Hunter!" Swann shouted.

They all put on their helmets. The bit of remaining snow inside Kelton's sent a fresh chill through his body. If he hadn't been wearing this helmet during the avalanche, he'd be dead. It had trapped what little air he had left when he was buried to prevent the snow from drowning him. Still, wearing it again reminded him of being helplessly encased in the bone-chilling black.

The cold. As Kelton followed, a distant third behind Hunter and Swann, the frigid wind cut through his wet snow-sodden clothes, freeze-stiffening the fabric and numbing parts of his body that before now had been mostly OK. His sled hit a bump, and he nearly fell off. If he couldn't warm himself, at least a little, he'd never be physically able to drive his snowmobile out of the backcountry. If he didn't get out of here, he could freeze to death.

"Come on, Hunter," Kelton whispered. "Please just find the mine. Hurry."

SWANN FOLLOWED HUNTER, BUT KEPT GLANCING BACK TO make sure Kelton was still behind her. The poor guy was hidden behind the visor of his helmet, but she didn't need to see his face to know he was miserable. He was hanging over the front of his snowmobile like a mannequin or a corpse. They'd tried to get the snow brushed off him and out of his clothes, but he didn't have the best snow- and water-resistant gear, and he had been ice-packed solid like the fresh-caught salmon her parents sometimes had shipped in back home at their old house.

"Oh, I wish we were in California now," Swann said quietly.

"Like, in the middle of July. This guy could use a hot day on the beach."

Hunter mostly led them back along their old tracks, but a few times he seemed to find a better course, routing them a different way around some mostly snowed-under trees or toward a more level path. A couple of times he stopped and looked around, their old tracks lost in the growing drifts of fresh snow.

Finally he stopped so long that Swann caught up to him. She flipped up her visor and shouted to him over their engine noise, "Where is it?"

"I don't . . . It's close!" Hunter shouted. He wasn't only yelling to be heard over the noise of the engine, but he sounded as frustrated as Swann was worried. "The woods look different on the way back. A tree or boulder is shaped one way when you look at it from one direction, but is completely different heading the other way, plus now everything is covered in more snow. And the farther we go, the older our trail, the harder it is to find. Our older tracks have been blown and snowed over, like someone took a giant eraser and wiped them out."

Swann bit her lip. This couldn't be happening. A few years ago, flipping through the channels, watching TV at her grandmother's house, Swann had found a show about some hunters being lost on a snowy mountain in Alaska. They had nearly died out in the snow before a helicopter could finally fly in to rescue them. Even then, the men were hospitalized with frostbite and hypothermia stuff. Was that what was happening to them? "Are you saying you're lost?"

"What?" Hunter glanced at Kelton as he pulled up on his snowmobile. "No! I just . . . Come on. Let's go."

They drove off again, and now Swann was sure they were completely off their old trail. Hunter was making this up as he went along. She was getting cold now herself. She hoped Hunter would make up the correct way to the mine soon.

But he didn't find it soon. The three of them worked their way back in the direction from which they'd come, moving up the mountain and then back down. Searching. Freezing. And it was getting harder to see out there as the snow picked up and the afternoon began to darken toward evening.

Swann checked behind her again and her heart jumped. Kelton's snowmobile was stopped. He'd fallen off and lay facedown in the snow. She shouted for Hunter, tried to wave, but he wasn't watching and couldn't hear her. "Oh no. Kelton, don't be dead."

She couldn't wait for Hunter to turn around and notice something was wrong. Kelton couldn't wait. She cranked her snowmobile around and sped back down the slope to stop beside Kelton. "Kelton!" She slid to her knees at Kelton's side and took hold of his shoulders, shaking him. "Come on, Kelton. Answer me!"

"I'm OK." He slid around in the snow, trying to get up. "Just so cold. D-don't know if I can get back on my sled."

This was turning into that rescue show. Only nobody knew the three of them were back here. Cynthia knew she was in the race, but was the race over yet? Would anyone even notice she hadn't turned up at the finish line? How long would it take people to realize something was wrong? Swann slid her arms under Kelton and tried to pull him up. He was a skinny guy, like most of the boys in her grade, but he was still heavy. "Come on, buddy. You have to help me here. Let's get on my snowmobile. I'll drive us both to the mine. Hunter's probably found it by now."

"No," Kelton mumbled. "Got t-take my—"

"No arguments," Swann said. "This is the only way."

"My stuff," Kelton mumbled. "Swann, wait a second . . ."

"It's OK," she assured him. "I got you."

It took a while, but she finally helped get him seated on her snowmobile. There was just enough room behind him for her to sit if they were close, and sitting close was the only way she was going to be able to keep him from falling off. With her arms on either side of Kelton, she hit the throttle again, and backtracked toward Hunter, trying to put on extra speed to catch up fast.

The problem was that on the way up the mountain, eventually a bunch of snowmobile tracks crossed in all directions, and it was impossible to be sure of the correct path after Hunter.

"Kelton, keep talking to me, OK?" Swann had no idea if this was one of those situations where a person going to sleep or passing out was a terrible problem, but sometimes in the movies or on TV people had to keep a victim awake. "Can you believe Hunter wasn't watching behind him and lost us? You guys don't get along so well, huh? I bet you're really mad at him now. What a jerk, huh? Is that what you think?"

"He's OK," Kelton said. "Shot a wolf."

"Yeah," Swann said. "I read about that in the school newspaper. Crazy stuff. I can't believe I live in a place with actual wolves."

"G-gotta . . . find that mine," Kelton said. "Or just a p-place for a f-fire."

"We'll get there," Swann said, trying to sound more confident than she felt. "We're almost there now."

A light shined from behind a big snowdrift ahead. Swann slowed down a little. Finally Hunter rode into view. He stopped, waved frantically at her, and turned around. He must have found the mine. Why else would he be so excited?

"I think Hunter's found it," Swann said. "We're almost there."

And finally, the three of them reached their temporary destination. The headlights from their two snowmobiles shining on a dark hole in the snow, big enough to walk inside if they ducked.

Parking just outside the cave, Hunter and Swann helped Kelton off the snowmobile and through the deep snow. "Seriously, a mine?" Swann asked. Kelton could barely walk. He slipped, and she nearly fell under his weight. "I mean, mines are in cowboy movies and stuff."

"Yeah," Hunter grunted. Swann felt a little better knowing he was struggling with Kelton too. "This is Idaho. Where do you think all that cowboy stuff happened?"

Swann turned her phone light on and they walked into a gently downward-sloping dark cave that had been chiseled into the mountain. Snow had blown in close to the entrance, and either some earlier snow had melted and refrozen or water had flowed inside some other way, because a lot of the floor was covered in a thick layer of ice.

"Careful," Swann said, her voice echoing a little in the cave. "It's slippery."

Hunter almost fell. "No kidding. Let's set him down here."

They eased Kelton to a sitting position with his back to the wall. The poor guy, slow and shaking, moved his arms to hug himself.

"Little warmer in here," Hunter said.

"And dark," Swann said. "Did you bring your phone?"

Hunter shook his head. "Like I said. No reception out here. Plus, it's kind of a nice phone and I didn't want to risk losing it." He shrugged. "Sorry, but this race wasn't supposed to last that long. I didn't know I'd need my phone for a light in a mine."

Kelton patted himself. "My ch-cheap phone. Must fallen outta my p-pocket in the avalanche."

"OK, forget the phones," Swann said, worrying at the sight of thirty-two percent battery remaining. She shivered. "We have to get a fire going somehow. Does anyone have any matches?" Only the wind whistling at the mine's entrance answered, the most frightening response she could have imagined. "Nobody? What are we going to do?" She started pacing, but slipped on the ice and nearly fell. "What did we come here for if we can't light a fire?" She could barely see the guys now. Darkness was falling outside, and coming on even faster in the mine.

"Emergency k-kit," Kelton said quietly. "On my s-sled. T-tried to tell you."

Swann looked out into the storm. She twisted a lock of hair around her finger, gazing into the deepening darkness.

"On his . . ." Hunter began. "We can't go back looking for his snowmobile. We barely found our way up here in the first place. We'll get lost out there with no cover at all."

"We have to try," Swann insisted.

Hunter sighed. "Do you know what people call this mountain? The old guys anyway?"

Swann folded her arms. "Mount McCall. Big McCall and Little McCall."

"That's what it says on the map. But the old hunters and trappers have passed on a different name. They call it Storm Mountain. It's something to do with the way moisture blows through the pass and the colder temperatures at elevation." Hunter shrugged. "I don't know. But tons of snow get dumped on this part of the mountain. Over a hundred years ago, the miners who were working up here were all caught in a freak early blizzard. They all froze to death or starved. Bad winter. Nobody could get up here to find the bodies until spring."

"Great," Swann said. "That's a real encouraging story, Hunter. So we're out of the snowmobile race. Now we're just racing Storm Mountain."

"Swann," Hunter tried.

"There is no other way," Swann said. "Without a fire, he'll

freeze. We all will. We need to bring his snowmobile up here. To do that, we both have to go."

"If we go out there, we could die," Hunter said.

Swann took a deep breath, getting ready to slide on her helmet. "If we don't go out, we'll almost certainly die."

CHAPTER 9

SWANN TOOK ONE LAST LOOK AT KELTON, SHIVERING ON the ground, before she pushed on her helmet and stepped out into the biting wind. Almost instantly, snow plastered her whole front side.

"It's so dark out here." Hunter shouted to be heard.

"Then we have to hurry," Swann called back. In two pulls, she'd started her snowmobile.

Hunter kind of raised a hand in objection. "Maybe I should—"

Swann jumped on the snowmobile, gripping the handlebars and giving the throttle a little boost to turn the machine around.

"Yeah, you drive," he finished, climbing on behind her.

A moment later they were out shredding the powder again. Swann drove her snowmobile faster than she had all day, abandoning caution and forgetting safety. She was feeling a little numb in her fingers and toes. The cold crept in everywhere. If she felt that bad, what must this be like for Kelton?

They hadn't been in the mine for very long, so they were

blessed with fresher snowmobile tracks to guide them, but it still wasn't easy. Like Hunter had said earlier, the landscape seemed to change depending on what direction one was traveling, and now the darkness and blowing snow made it even more of a challenge. She slowed down, but only a little.

Finally she hit the brake and skidded to a halt.

"What?" Hunter asked.

Swann had almost missed it too. The snowdrift on their left had just a few gaps, revealing Kelton's snowmobile underneath. "The snow's blowing in fast!" she called to Hunter. "A few more minutes, and it would be totally buried." She got up and started brushing the snow off the machine.

Hunter helped. When it was mostly cleared off, he flipped up the seat, revealing the compartment underneath, packed with extra clothes and a few plastic bags filled with different supplies. Swann hadn't even known snowmobiles had storage space like that. Hunter slammed the seat back into place. "Kelton has been talking about this snowmobile forever. How he's been working on it. Let's hope he did a good job and we can get it started and back to the mine."

"If not, we'll just take the stuff back with us," Swann said.

But in four pulls, Hunter had Kelton's snowmobile started.

"Let's get back there," said Swann. "I hope we're in time."

After another hard ride to the mine, they found Kelton had rolled or fallen over on his side and lay there curled up in a little ball.

For a moment Swann was terrified he was dead, but then

she saw him shivering, and she rushed to his side. "Kelton, we're back. We brought your snowmobile." She glanced out into the dark where Hunter had gone. "Hunter's bringing your stuff. You have matches or something?"

"Innabagsh," Kelton said. He groaned as he struggled to get up. "Gotta lighter inder."

Hunter returned, shining a flashlight up in his face the way some people did when telling scary stories. "Flashlight. Good call, Kelton."

"It'll give my phone light a rest, save the battery," Swann added.

Hunter continued, "Plus, looks like a lighter, a rope, some bandage stuff, and in this other bag, dry socks, sweatshirt, and sweatpants. Fresh gloves."

"That ain't it. You trynta hog it all," Kelton said.

"Dude." Hunter pulled a Snickers bar out of his pocket. "I wasn't going to eat it myself."

"Forget the candy," Swann said. "We have a lighter. Let's get a fire going."

"Burning what?" Hunter asked. "Trees out there all covered with snow."

Swann reached for the flashlight and Hunter handed it over. "You help him change into his dry clothes. I'll see if there's anything in this mine we can burn."

"Why should I have to help him with his clothes?" Hunter asked.

"Are you serious right now?" Swann said. "It'd be weird if

I did it." Kelton already had his gloves off and was fumbling helplessly with the zipper on his coat. "Just help him, Hunter!"

"Well, keep the light over here, then!"

Swann kept the light on Kelton so Hunter could see what he was doing, but she looked around the cave. About twelve feet back from the entrance, a second cave branched out in shadow off the main tunnel. How big was this mine? "I can't believe we're in a real mine, that it's just out here, for no reason. No fence or anything."

"Might have been a fence—Kelton, can you push your hand through, yeah, through the sleeve there?—before. Maybe some old barbed-wire fence, wooden fence posts rotted out and the whole thing buried in the snow."

"OK, but if they're so dangerous, why didn't someone just fill this in?" Swann asked. She risked a look behind her. Hunter was getting Kelton into dry sweatpants.

"There's another mine not far past the fence behind my family's hunting property, on state land. My grandpa said he'd destroy my whole life if he ever found out I'd tried to go down in it. But he talked about an article he read about abandoned Idaho mines. There are abandoned mines all over the state. Some government group was guessing there could be thousands more they don't know about."

"Thanks, Hunter," Kelton said quietly. "K-kind of em-embarrassing needing help to—"

"No big deal," Hunter said quickly.

Swann swung the flashlight around, checking out the side

tunnel. "I wonder what's in—" She stopped. The branch line didn't go far off the entrance. It was some kind of storage room. The rock wall had a natural or carved-in stone ledge with a wooden shelf upon it, and resting on that, a wooden box. "In here. At least one thing we can burn." She stepped closer and started rubbing the dust off the side of the crate. "It's pretty dirty," she called back to the guys.

"Well," Hunter said, joining her in the storage chamber, "this will be a start."

Swann brushed more dust. "Hey, something written on the box. Dangerous. High . . . explo . . ." She trailed off staring at the word EXPLOSIVES. She was about to brush off more dust when Hunter caught her hand.

"Hey, Swann," he whispered, gently tugging at her arm. "We probably shouldn't mess with this."

"Why are you whispering?"

Hunter pulled her all the way back to Kelton. He still spoke quietly. "There's some type of explosives in that box. Dynamite. Maybe black powder. Grandpa said sometimes people find old blasting caps in mines like this."

"So?"

"So?" Hunter said. "For all we know, that stuff's been here a hundred years or more."

"It doesn't look like anyone's messed with it," Swann said. "Been sitting on a dry shelf. It's not like we're going to light the fuses or anything."

"That's what I said to my grandpa when he was talking about

this. He owns a construction company, does a lot of roadwork. Sometimes his company has to blast rock out of the way. The stuff they use is modern and a lot better. He said the stuff they had for mining in the old cowboy times wasn't even very good back then. And when it gets older, it can just go off if people mess with it."

"What do you mean, mess with it?" Swann asked, glancing nervously back at the storage tunnel.

Hunter shrugged. "I don't know. Maybe my grandfather talked more about it, but I wasn't paying attention. He just said, like, it could go off easily. Maybe if it gets bumped too much?"

"Maybe?" Swann said.

Kelton shivered on the ground near the entrance to the mine.

"What should we do?" Hunter asked.

"We need the wood," Swann whispered. "If we don't get Kelton warmed up, he could die."

"But the explosives," Hunter protested.

"We'll move the box out of the way and take the board from underneath it. Maybe the dynamite or whatever will explode." She gave Hunter a playful pretend punch to the shoulder and smiled. "Maybe it won't." She handed the flashlight to Hunter. "You hold the flashlight. I'll move the box."

"But I should be the one to—"

Before Hunter could go on about how it was his job as a boy to risk himself, she slapped the flashlight into his hand and went to the storage chamber. There she approached the high explosives box. She let out a deep breath. *I'm supposed to be in*

L.A. I should be surfing right now. Or at a cello lesson. Anything besides messing with boxes of explosives from pioneer times. Swann fought to keep her hands from shaking as she reached out and took hold of the ropes on either side of the box. "I'm going to move the box now, Hunter," Swann whispered. "You might want to step back, just in case . . . you know."

"Swann," Hunter whispered. "If anything blows up down here . . . it won't matter where we're standing in the mine."

Swann swallowed. "Oh yeah." Very gently, holding her breath, hands sweating, she carefully lifted the crate off the shelf. She'd expected it to be heavier, but then she had no idea how much dynamite weighed. When nothing happened, she slowly and evenly stepped back. One step. Another. The edge of the crate cleared the shelf. If she dropped the box now . . . She bit her lip. There was no time to think about that. Finally, she'd lifted the crate clear.

Hunter beamed the flashlight inside it.

The box was empty. Even so, Swann let out her breath slowly.

"Well, that was a lot of fuss over nothing." Hunter was still whispering.

"Yeah," Swann said aloud. "And we're wasting time. Let's get anything that can burn out there to get a fire going."

Moments later she was back in the entry chamber, working to unseal Kelton's plastic bag with her cold numb fingers. "Kelton, you there?" she said as she pulled out a lighter and some scraps of cardboard.

"Y-yeah," Kelton said. "Just so cold. You gotta make, like,

a pyramid out of the cardboard, right by the wood. B-better to break that box up into s-smaller s-splinters."

Although the empty explosives crate was super-old, it was still pretty solid. Swann leaned it against a rock by the wall and stomped it, busting it under her boot. She kept stomping the pieces smaller and smaller until she figured that had to be enough, then set to work arranging the bits around the cardboard.

"You want t-to g-get it shaped like—"

Swann turned away from her work. "I've seen them build fires in the movies. I'm not totally helpless, you know."

But when it came time to light the cardboard, the lighter wouldn't work. She kept pressing the button, but absolutely nothing happened. "Oh no," she breathed. If this lighter wouldn't work, it would be a dangerous-cold night for all of them.

"What's the problem?" Kelton asked.

Swann pressed the button again and again. "This worthless . . . it won't work! It doesn't do anything!" She held the lighter up before him and pressed the little button on top. "I keep pressing the . . ." She trailed off as Kelton started shaking even more than he had been. "What's the matter? Are you OK?" Was he going into some kind of hypothermic shock? "Kelton? Talk to me."

"I can't breathe," Kelton gasped as he shook.

Swann put her hands on his shoulders. Was he dying? "What's the matter? What can I do?"

Kelton sucked in a huge breath. "You can flick your finger along that silver wheel at the top!"

Swann frowned. He was OK? "Are you . . . are you laughing at me?" A strange mix of annoyance and relief swirled inside her. He was laughing. It had returned some color to his cheeks.

"Oh my gosh. SuperPop! Have you ever used a lighter?"

She shoved Kelton's shoulder. "Shut up! Of course I've used a lighter. But not this kind. My father let me use a kind of almost gun-shaped lighter to light a gas fireplace once. What's the big deal? I just pulled the black trigger or button or whatever and it clicked and fire came out the end. This button doesn't even click."

Kelton held his glove over his mouth and squinted his eyes as though trying to contain his laughter. "It's OK. I get it. Different backgrounds."

"I'm not helpless!" She was trying to help him and he was laughing at her like she was stupid. Who did this . . . this weirdo think he was?

"I know you're not," Kelton said. "You didn't grow up with smokers in the house and lighters all over. I get it." He nodded toward the lighter. "You gotta flick your thumb down that silver wheel real quick, then hold that button down. While you hold the button down, fire will keep coming out."

"Well, how was I supposed to know?" Swann flicked on the lighter and held the little yellow flame to a the edge of a piece of cardboard, which darkened and curled. She lit another piece and a third. Swann watched carefully, desperately hoping the little bits of wood would ignite. She helped by flicking the lighter on a thin splinter, holding the flame there until the tan wood darkened. Had the fire caught? Was the splinter burning? This had to work.

"Swann," Kelton said from behind her.

"What?" she said sharply. "What else am I doing wrong?"

"I'm sorry," he said quietly.

She spun away from the growing fire, the flickering flames dancing patterns of shadow and light around the room and around Kelton. "For what? The avalanche wasn't—"

"I didn't mean to make fun of you about the lighter."

The only thing worse than mockery from a guy like Kelton Fielding was his pity. She shrugged. "I don't care."

"I know," he said, edging closer to the fire. "Still, it was mean. Rich people probably don't use cheap lighters like that. Why would you have used one?"

She wanted to argue against the idea that she was any different from him just because her parents were wealthier, but she knew a lot about McCall, Idaho, and a little about Kelton's background—enough to know there were certain differences in the way they lived. "I'm not a stupid useless rich girl."

"Naw," Kelton said. "It wasn't stupid."

Swann rolled her eyes, and turned back toward the growing flames, feeling the heat flaring against her cheeks.

CHAPTER 10

IRON MIKE STEPPED INTO THE BEAR STONE BREWERY, stomping his boots in the entryway, not that it mattered. During Winter Carnival, so many snowy people came in and out of this place that the wood floor was quite a wet mess. He tugged his beard, frustrated that his early search had come up fruitless, and not happy about what he had to do here at Bear Stone.

"Iron Mike!" Eddie Ferson, a guy at the bar who'd graduated a few years after Mike, whom everyone called Fireball, raised a glass.

"Fireball." Mike stepped up close to him. He was a big snowmobile and ski man. "You good? Not too many drinks?"

Fireball looked at him like he was crazy. "Not even one sip. I just got here."

Mike patted his shoulder. "Get some reliable men, guys you can trust, who know their way around snowmobiles and the area. No tourists or amateurs. We need a solid search party out on checkpoint one of the snowmobile racecourse. We got three missing kids. Sheriff Hamlin's setting up the search."

"In the dark?" Fireball asked. "All this snow?"

Mike shrugged. "It's bad. I know. That's why we need to hurry. This storm's got aircraft grounded, so we can't get a helo up with infrared to scan for their heat signatures."

Fireball was on his feet. "Yeah, I'll round up the guys, but you didn't have to come here. Coulda called me."

Mike looked over to a table on the other side of the restaurant where Josie Abbott was taking an order. "Josie's boy is one of the missing."

Fireball's usual excited look dropped. "Oh. You came here to tell her."

"Those new actors who come to town? Their daughter, Swann, is missing too. And my nephew Hunter."

"Aw, man. Sorry. Figure they're together?"

Don't know. Mike clenched his fists, keeping himself together. "Hope so. Now I better go tell the kid's mom."

Fireball slapped Mike on the arm, threw a couple of bills on the bar, and left his drink behind untouched, already making calls to get more search help.

Mike headed across the place, his boots thumping heavy on the wood floor. Josie laughed with the customers at the table she'd just been helping and turned around to head back toward the kitchen, stopping just short of running into Mike.

"Iron Mike," she said, surprised. "Sorry about that. Excuse me. Have a seat anywhere. You know the drill."

"Hey, Josie," he said. Her smile faded at the sound of the cold serious tone in Mike's voice. "I got some bad news. You might want to sit down."

Josie Abbott was another who'd graduated a few years after Mike. He didn't know her too well, but word got around in small towns like McCall, and he knew she'd had a challenging time in life. Apparently her difficulties had toughened her, because she did not sit down and didn't crumble.

"Is he dead?" she asked seriously.

A loud man who'd been drinking too much whistled. "Hey, honey, I been waiting for another round for—"

"Shut your mouth or get out!" she yelled at him.

"Kelton's missing," Mike explained. "So's my nephew Hunter and the daughter of that actor, girl named Swann Siddiq."

Josie shook her head. "What? That doesn't make sense. Kelton doesn't hang around with—"

"They were in the snowmobile race. All three of them cleared the first checkpoint, but didn't show up for the next one."

She let out a tired, frustrated sigh. "That stupid snowmobile. All that boy's cared about lately. I can't believe he's done this."

"You didn't know he was in the race?" Mike asked.

Josie held her hands out. "Been kind of busy." But she wasn't busy anymore. She took off her apron and marched over to the owner, Jason, behind the bar, saying something Mike couldn't hear over the music and conversation.

"Come on, Josie," Jason said. "Look at this place. I'm swamped here."

"Jason, my son is missing! I've been working here five years, never missed a shift, covered for everybody else! Now you will let me go find my boy or I'm done here!"

Jason held up his hands. "I'm sorry. I didn't know. Yes, of course, go find Kelton. We'll be praying."

Josie nodded, then spun to face Mike. "Let's go get my boy."

"YOU CAN'T KEEP A SECRET THIS LONG," YUMI EXPLAINED to Annette. The two of them had set up an awesome sleepover out at the lodge with a roaring fire in the woodstove, cheesy old movies on TV, and a ridiculous amount of delicious but unhealthy snacks. "It's against the friendship code."

Annette laughed. "Oh, sorry! I've heard of *The Da Vinci Code*, but not the friendship code. Is it any good?"

Yumi threw a cheese puff at Annette. Annette rescued the treat from her hair and chomped down on it. "Anyway, I don't even know if I like him as much anymore. There might . . . kind of . . . be someone else."

"You would cheat on the Mysterious Secret Crush?" Yumi faked outrage.

They'd been sitting up on the island countertop in the kitchen. If Grandpa had caught them like that, he probably would have had them both stuffed like Reagan, his prized taxidermized bear. As if reading Yumi's thoughts, Annette slid off the counter down to the floor, pacing the room. "I can't cheat on someone if I've barely talked to him."

Yumi rolled her eyes. "Fine, if you won't tell me who the Mysterious Secret Crush is, then tell me who the other guy is."

Annette spun to face her. "Not a chance in—" The lights

flickered. Then everything shut off, submerging the girls in deep darkness.

"Oh crap," Yumi said. "All that snow. Tree must have fallen on the lines."

"What do we do?" Annette said. She sounded worried.

Yumi's eyes had adapted to the faint glow coming from the stove. "We put some more wood in the furnace and get some blankets over there. We'll be plenty warm. Don't worry. There'll be just enough light to play cards or Monopoly or something."

"No Monopoly, thanks," Annette said. "You play too seriously."

Yumi shrugged and took the old-fashioned corded telephone handset off its claw hook thing on the wall, holding it to her ear for a moment. "Yep. Dead. And forget cell service out here, especially in a storm. We'll just have to hang out and talk about your secret crush."

"Yeah." Annette flew in out of nowhere and whapped Yumi hard with a pillow. "Or I get my revenge for your spying with the pillow of death!"

The girls exchanged a few pillow strikes before collapsing in laughter, secure in the warm cabin, apart from the world.

"YOU GUYS OUGHT TO SEE THIS PLACE!" HUNTER SAID, returning to the entrance chamber with an armload of boards. "I went a little deeper into the mine, found more wood. The tunnel goes on forever. Do you think there's any gold left? That would be awesome."

"Y-yeah, Higgins," Kelton said. "They abandoned the mine because there w-was tons of gold to be found." The warmth from the fire pushed through his body in waves, like a living thing.

It was hard to see with Swann turning toward Hunter, hiding her face in shadows, but he had the sense she wasn't happy. Was she still mad about him laughing at her? Idiot thing to do. He was always doing idiot things.

"Are you serious right now?" Swann said. "Gold? Hunter, we're in big trouble here."

Kelton bit his lip. It wasn't often he saw a Popular like Hunter Higgins looking so embarrassed. For a long time they all were quiet. The wind moaned through the mine. The fire crackled.

Finally, Hunter brought the wood over by the fire, huddling close on the other side. "I want to let this get burning stronger before I put on any more wood." He shivered. "Man, it's cold. And I wasn't even buried in the snow."

"Thanks for digging me out, you two," Kelton said. How had he not thanked them until now? They'd saved his life. For real. "I would have . . . I mean . . ."

"We couldn't just leave you down there," Swann said. "What do you think we are?"

They were Populars. He didn't just think that. He knew it. Well, in Swann's case a SuperPop. They weren't generally people who cared about guys like him. But they weren't monsters.

"Well, I didn't think you'd intentionally let me die down there, even if I am a Grit."

"A what?" Swann pulled her legs up against her chest and wrapped her arms around them, sitting near him by the fire.

"A Grit—" Kelton started to explain.

"It's the word he uses for people he thinks get picked on," Hunter said.

"No," Kelton shot back. The fire was warming him now, but he felt even hotter due to the way Hunter sounded like he was making fun of what he'd said. Like how a couple of Mom's old boyfriends had sounded when Kelton had tried to talk to them about something that had happened at school, and they didn't care because they thought it was just dumb kids' stuff. "See, I'm a Grit, one of those people who doesn't have anything. And you two are Populars, or Pops, people whose parents just give them everything they want, people who run the whole school because everybody, including the teachers, thinks you're so awesome."

Hunter shook his head. Swann looked at him wide-eyed. "Is that how you see me?"

Kelton was careful not to laugh. "You're something more. You're a SuperPopular, SuperPop. All famous and stuff. Not even on the same scale."

"My parents don't just hand me everything I want," Hunter said.

"I can't help it if my parents have been successful," Swann said sharply. "It doesn't make me a bad person."

Kelton held his hands up. "I didn't say it did. Just that we're kind of from different worlds, you and me."

"Seems like we're both from McCall now," Swann said.

Hunter snorted, leaning back against the rock wall of the entryway cavern. Kelton had no idea how he could stand to be that far from the warmth of the fire. "Well, right now," Hunter said, "we're all from a crappy, freezing-cold abandoned mine in the middle of nowhere." He added, under his breath, "Thanks to someone's so-called shortcut."

"I didn't invite either of you along with me," Kelton said. He clenched his fists, grateful he was able, once again, to do so. "I told you to go back! But no. Why listen to me? I'm just a Grit."

"Oh, would you stop with that?" Swann said. "You'd be dead if not for us."

Kelton put another shard of the wooden crate on the fire. "If Hunter or some other Pop had thought of my idea, nobody would be saying it was bad."

"You really believe that, don't you?" Hunter said. "All that us-versus-them stuff? Like all your problems are everybody else's fault? Never your own?"

Kelton had had about as much as he could take from this Popular. "What? It's my fault I've never lived in the same home longer than two years? My fault when business at the restaurant slows down and they cut my mom's hours so she gets behind on the bills? My fault when her boyfriends waste her money on stupid spoiler-wing-things for their cars instead of on rent?"

"That's not what I—"

All of these ideas had been boiling in Kelton for so long, and now that he'd almost died and could still die trying to get out of this snowy trap, he felt a tremendous release of energy, like an unwinding of a rubber band that's been twisted and twisted by all of life's crap over the years. "I remember. . . . Christmas. Like first grade. We were friends back then, remember?"

Hunter looked away and all was quiet for a moment. Finally he spoke up. "I don't think we stopped being—"

"Yeah, right, Hunter. We got older, and you realized I was a Grit and then you didn't want to hang out anymore." Kelton shrugged. "It's OK. I get it. This isn't a you-have-to-be-my-friend pity party. Just stating facts. Christmas. First grade. We'd been hanging out, watching TV. Saw a commercial for an electric racetrack. Remember that? It had all the lights and sound effects? Looked so awesome. And we'd learned enough about numbers and the internet to be able to look it up and find out it cost over a hundred bucks. Which we both asked our parents and they both kind of put us off, saying it was real expensive. Then the idea hit us! It didn't matter how much the racetrack cost because we could just ask Santa Claus. Wrote my letter to Santa asking for that one thing, that racetrack. As long as you're good and make the nice list, you're golden. Right? Oh, I was so good. I did everything the teachers said. I figured out where all the brushes and rags were kept so I could clean stuff at home. Even scrubbed the toilets. I didn't whine. Didn't complain. You actually got grounded for a few days after Thanksgiving for something. But Christmas morning, I got socks and a pack of those old-fashioned cheap plastic Army men. You got the racetrack."

"Oh, so you're mad because you didn't get a toy when we were kids? Santa Claus didn't come through for you, so—"

"No!" Kelton's shout echoed through the cavern and they all looked around, a little worried. In the movies and on TV, loud noises could cause cave-ins and avalanches. He quieted himself. "It just shows how that your-problems-are-all-your-own-fault idea is crap. They told us be good and get on the nice list and good things would happen. They basically still tell us that. Only I always end up with nothing. And guys like you, Hunter? The Populars? You always get everything. Always have. Like this race. Your dad just gave you that snowmobile to ride. I had to pawn my mom's ex-boyfriend's knife to pay for my entry fee and for parts to get my sled running, and now I won't be able to pay him back. You two don't have any problems like that at all."

"You're so full of crap, Fielding," Hunter said. "I'm sorry that your mom has money trouble, but that's not my fault—"

"Never said it was!" Kelton said.

"And you do bring a lot of your own troubles on yourself." Hunter kept talking. "Like in Ms. Foudy's class, you always tap my shoulder wanting to talk about whatever. Keep getting us both in trouble."

"Oh, I thought we were still friends," Kelton said. "Just friends that can never talk? And if that's what you think is a big problem . . ." He laughed sadly. "I wish I had your problems. Instead of thawing out a frozen pizza or microwaving a frozen burrito, it would be nice to sit down to a family meal. You Richies and Pops have no idea—"

"You're wrong, though, Kelton," Swann said quietly. "I'm richer—" She stopped herself, eyes closed. "My *parents* are richer than both of your families combined." She shrugged. "Sorry. That's just the truth. There's nothing I can do about it. But it's been forever since I sat down to a meal with my parents. They moved us way out here to—"

"Way out here?" Hunter said. "This is our home."

"And mine too now," Swann said. "Sorry. I just meant my parents took me out of my old school, away from everyone I know, so we could get in touch with nature or our true selves and stuff, and I don't know anyone, and then they're gone all the time, back to L.A. or some location for shoots or publicity. I spend more time with my babysitter than with them."

Swann's words hung in the air for a long moment.

"I thought she was your au pair," Kelton said.

All three of them laughed. It was a welcome small break in the tension. Kelton slipped three more pieces of wood onto the fire. It was burning very well now, and it was quite hot beside it. He backed up a little to find the sweet spot between the heat of the fire and the freezing cold of the snowy wind blowing into the mine.

"I spend more time with Cynthia than with my parents," said Swann. "The whole reason I'm stuck here in this mine is . . ." She shook her head and turned away from them, wiping her eyes. "So stupid," she mumbled.

"I don't think it's stupid to enter the race," Hunter said.

"I thought if I won this race, then maybe . . . You know my father was supposed to award the prize at the finish line."

"You thought if you won, you'd get your dad's attention," Kelton said.

Swann looked up at him, and their eyes met. He wanted to tell her he'd signed up for basically the same reasons, that he'd wanted to prove he wasn't a total loser, that he could do good in at least one thing. But Hunter would make fun of him. Or he'd tell the guys at school and they'd make fun of him.

He somehow doubted Swann would mock him, but you could never tell with a SuperPop. She was the daughter of people who acted for a living. She was probably acting now. For real.

Swann smiled at him for a moment, just briefly, so that the gesture was almost lost in the flickering light, but in that moment, Kelton felt a tingle very different from the cold shivers he'd experienced all night.

They were quiet for a long time. A howling wind blew snow and ice in at them, as though the storm were a living thing, clawing at the cave to get at them, to freeze them all out.

"Well, we're going to need more wood," Hunter finally said. "This is all going to burn up quick." He started back down the tunnel.

"Hunter, you really shouldn't be going all around in here," Kelton said.

"Yeah," said Hunter. "I watched the same mines-are-dangerous video you saw in class. But we need wood, or it won't just be you freezing. All the wood outside is going to be soaked, covered in snow, or so green it will hardly burn and will just smoke us out anyway."

"A rocky old mine doesn't seem like the best source of firewood either," Swann said. "What are we going to do?"

Hunter nodded down the tunnel. "I think I saw an old wood ladder way back there. Kind of falling apart. I'll bring back pieces of that."

"I'd go with you," Kelton said. "But I can hardly move."

"I'll come with you," Swann said.

Kelton felt more reluctant for Swann to go than he thought he would, but it was also true that none of them should be going very deep into the mine. "These tunnels can be unstable. You don't want to go knocking stuff around too much."

"We don't want to freeze to death either," Hunter fired back.

Swann patted Kelton's shoulder. "Stay here. Warm up. Keep the fire going. We'll be back soon."

Kelton felt her hand on his shoulder long after she and Hunter had disappeared into the shadows again. Maybe he should have gone with them. But he was only now getting feeling back in his hands and feet, a process which was actually a little painful, and someone had to tend the fire. Still, it bothered him to see the two of them go off together, to hear their voices, a little laughter, echoing from the dark. The Populars off together, and Kelton, as always, left alone.

From outside the mine came a shrieking howl. A coyote, probably. He hoped it was the sound of a coyote and not a wolf.

Another howl answered the first. What could possibly be out there in this snow?

A moment later another howl, a scream, came from deeper in the mine.

"Swann?" Kelton shouted.

Hunter screamed, but this was wrong, a shout of fear and pain. Some kind of thudding, crunching sound. Then Swann screamed, even louder than before.

"What's going on?" Kelton called. "You guys OK?"

"Kelton!" came the sound of Swann's voice. "Oh my gosh, Kelton! Get back here! Hurry! Hunter fell down a . . . fell down a thing! Hurry! I think he might be dead."

CHAPTER 11

SWANN DID A KIND OF STUTTER STEP BACK-AND-FORTH toward the hole and away from it. "Nonononooo. Hunter?" Only the faintest glow shined up from the flashlight on the ground next to Hunter's body—next to Hunter—so that near-total darkness surrounded Swann. She took out her phone for light, but somehow now it didn't seem to do much to push back the dark. Hunter had spotted some wood in the chamber below and tried to use the old ladder to get down there. It broke to pieces not long after he put his full weight on it, and he'd dropped right down. He lay on his back down there, eyes closed, leg at a weird angle. Was he breathing? "No, please don't be dead," she whispered, wiping her eyes. "Kelton, where are you?"

"Swann? Hunter?" Kelton's voice echoed through the darkness. "How am I supposed to find you?" He yelled and cursed. "I'm OK. Just tripped. Swann, I think there's more than one way to go. You gotta direct me."

"Kelton," Swann called back. "Hunter is . . . he's not answering. His eyes are closed. He has the flashlight. I only have my phone light. As long as we are all being honest tonight, I don't want to be one of those weak, frightened, fragile rich princess types who need to be rescued. But I am freaking out right now."

"Hey," Kelton's voice came from the black. "OK, Swann? We're good. Well, we're not good, but hang in there. I'm coming to help. I have my whole emergency kit. I got the lighter so I can kind of see, but I need you to tell me which way to go until I'm able to see your phone light."

What was he talking about? "I don't know. Hunter was leading the way." She hadn't been paying super-close attention to their route. "But I guess there aren't that many turns."

"Can you remember?"

"If you shut up and let me think about it!" Swann closed her eyes to concentrate, not that it made much of a difference. Dark was dark. "Let's see," she said quietly to herself. "Main chamber, splits to right and left at back." She added, louder to Kelton. "Are you to the back of the first tunnel yet?"

"Yeah."

"Turn right," Swann said. "And you're not going to like this next part but just shut up and listen. I don't know how far we went down the second tunnel, but Hunter was talking. About you. Start walking while I try to say what he was saying."

"Seriously?" Kelton's voice came from the dark. Did he sound closer? It was impossible to tell inside the echoing tunnels.

"Just do it, Kelton!" Swann said. "Hunter said something

like . . . Man, that Kelton. Um, I don't know what happened to him. Or something like that. He said he knew you, um, had some problems at home." Swann's cheeks flared hot. This was the worst thing to have to do, but it was the only way she could think to measure how long it took Hunter to lead her to this chamber.

"I think you're getting louder," Kelton said. "Maybe I'm closer?"

Swann clapped her hands. His voice was definitely closer. "Then he started talking about how . . ." She couldn't say this next part. Hunter had joked and complained about how Kelton always tapped his shoulder during study time. "He started talking about the two of you were friends and that you used to hang out more. And—" She could see something! "Hey! There's some light! I think I see you! Just barely, but there's something besides total darkness out there. Keep going."

She peered into the dark toward where she saw the light. But a moment later, all was total blackness again. "Or maybe not. I thought I saw light, but now it's gone."

A chuckle came out of the dark. A moment later the dim glow returned. "You see me. I was just burning my finger walking with the flame going on this lighter. I think I see your phone light."

"Should I come to you?" Swann asked.

"No!" Kelton said sharply. "Stay right where you are or we'll never find the hole where Hunter fell."

A moment later, the most wonderful sight, a little yellow

flame, and then Kelton's face with a nod and grim smile. "Hey. Sorry I took so long. Where's Hunter?"

KELTON LOOKED AT SWANN, WHO HAD SHUT OFF HER phone light to save the battery. Only faint light made her visible, shining up from below. She said nothing, but pointed at a small hole in the floor of the chamber. As Kelton Fielding stared at that hole, time seemed to slow down and the air in the mine grew colder, heavy somehow. He shivered and shook a little with dizziness as hundreds of thought fragments swirled through his mind.

Trapped. Getting home? Dead? Frostbite. His own fault. Dead? Collapse. His fault. Dead?

"Kelton?"

The fear shaking in Swann's voice hit Kelton like a slap in the face.

He rushed to the hole. On the rocky floor below, surrounded by bits of the collapsed old ladder, Hunter Higgins lay next to the flashlight with his eyes closed and his leg at an unnatural angle. "Hunter!" Kelton shouted. Who cared if loud noises could destabilize old mines? The guy was in trouble. After a moment's hesitation, Kelton dropped the rope from his emergency kit to the chamber floor, slipped on his gloves, and grabbed the two upright poles of what had been the ladder. A few rungs remained attached to either side. They'd slow his slide.

"Kelton, what are you doing?" Swann said. "You can't go down there. How will—"

Kelton did his best to wrap his hands and ankles around the poles, squeezing tight as he slid, still too fast, down the poles until his feet hit the rock, sending a sharp tingle through his legs. He wasted no time but dropped to his hands and knees next to Hunter, his ear over Hunter's nose and mouth.

A tingle of air on his ear and cheek. Kelton heaved a sigh.

"He's alive," he said. Kelton had never experienced a sense of relief like that ever before. A weight of terror and guilt had pressed in from all sides inside his chest and head, and now, with the release from the realization that he hadn't led his old friend to his death, he felt a lightening, almost like he could float them both out of here.

"Oh thank God," Swann said from above. She was crouched over the hole now, looking down on them.

"But that was a heck of a fall," Kelton said. "He could be hurt real bad. We have to be careful."

"What can we do if he's hurt?" Swann said. "We need a doctor."

Kelton fixed his gaze on her. "There might not be time. And we gotta figure the chance that nobody is coming for us. I mean, by now they're probably searching for us, but if we don't get out of this mine, it'll take them forever to find us."

"How are you going to get back up here?" Swann asked. "How will you get him up here? Or should I go try to find him some help?"

"Nobody's leaving anybody," Kelton said, sure of that one thing, at least.

"Then how—"

"First I gotta help Hunter. I watched a video about this kind of thing."

"You watch a lot of videos," Swann said quietly.

"Yeah, well . . ." How could he explain this without sounding pathetic or like he was begging for a friend? "I'm independent. Mom works late some nights. I'm alone a lot." He shook his head. *Focus, Kelton!* "I need to remember the steps. Check for responsiveness. He's out. Check breathing. Good. Now I have to look for bleeding."

"Bleeding? What kind of video did you watch?"

Kelton looked the guy over. He checked the dusty rock floor around Hunter's body. All dry. No blood. "It was like an Army thing. But it's still good. Except . . ."

"Except what?" Swann asked. "This is the worst! I feel so helpless. I'm coming down."

"No!" Kelton rose upright on his knees and pointed at her. "Stay up there. You come down, we may never get out of this mine. Ever." When Swann seemed to accept that, he turned his attention back to Hunter. "The problem with the Army video is that it was telling how to take care of soldiers a guy might find down on a battlefield."

"Which this isn't," Swann said. "Though maybe a war would be better."

"I'm supposed to gently slide my hands under his body, like slide them under his shoulders, then pull them out and check for blood on my hands. Then push my hands under him a little farther down his back, check for blood."

"But all of that's, like, for if a bullet ripped through his clothes," Swann said.

Kelton frowned, watching Hunter breathe. "Won't help us much now."

"That leg," said Swann.

"Has to be broken," Kelton said. "But the neck is the big deal here. If his neck or spine are cracked, and I move him, I could paralyze him."

"Well, how do you check for that?" Swann asked, a hint of panic rising in her voice.

"I don't know. The video didn't talk about that much. And in the movies they always put a foam collar thing around his neck."

Hunter moved his head a little, licking his lips. He took a deeper breath. Then he winced, as if in pain, squeezing his eyes shut and groaning. "My leg. Oh gaw . . . My leg."

"Hunter, buddy," Kelton said. "Hey, man, I'm right here with you. Can you hear me?"

Hunter opened his eyes wide, tears welling up. "Hurts, hurts. It hurts. It hurts."

Kelton leaned over Hunter's face. "Hunter, stop. Easy. I know it hurts. Breathe deep, and don't move. The old ladder busted apart. You fell. Been out cold."

"Kelton?" Hunter asked.

Kelton smiled. "You know who I am. That's a good sign."

"You'll be OK, Hunter," Swann called down to them. "Kelton watched a whole video about this stuff, and he knows how to help you."

"My leg . . ." Hunter groaned and bit his lip, tears rolling down his temples. He tried to tilt his head back, but Kelton held him in place.

"Hunter, you have to stay still." Kelton spoke kind of loudly, trying to get through Hunter's wall of pain. "That's gotta hurt bad, but you must stay still. For real."

"M'kay," Hunter said, still biting his lower lip and breathing hard through his nose.

"Can you wiggle your fingers?" Kelton asked. Hunter's gloved fingers wiggled. "Good. Can you wiggle your toes?" Hunter's feet were in boots, so Kelton was glad when Hunter grunted the affirmative. "Can you move your good leg a little?" Hunter's right leg moved.

"What about a concussion or something?" Swann asked.

"Right," Kelton said. He should have thought of that himself. "Hunter, do you know where you are?"

"I'm stuck in a freezing mine annnnnn," Hunter groaned. His eyes rolled back, and Kelton thought he'd pass out. But Hunter kept talking, rattling off his age, the date, the name of the president of the United States, his address.

"His head checks out," Kelton said. But Hunter's left leg was a mess. "I think we can risk moving you, Hunter. We need to get your snowmobile suit off. Check if your leg's bleeding. It's broken, but if it's one of those breaks where the bone comes out through the skin, you could be bleeding out inside your suit."

"It doesn't feel like it," Hunter said.

"I'm not sure you can tell, with all the pain." He took hold of the zipper near Hunter's collar, but Hunter put his hands on Kelton's, tears in his eyes. "I don't know if I can do it. It hurts so bad."

"Come on, Higgins," Kelton said. "You know I have to do this."

Slowly, Hunter's hands fell away, and Kelton unzipped and pulled the suit down to his waist. "This part ain't gonna feel too good. Stick with me, Higgins." As he started to pull the snowmobile suit down farther, moving Hunter's legs, the guy's face went red as he held in a scream. "That's good, man. We don't want to be yelling too much in an old mine." Once he had the one-piece jumpsuit off, he felt a brief surge of panic when he spotted the blood on Kelton's lower right leg where the bottom of his jeans was pushed up.

"What?" Hunter said. He must have recognized the look of fear in Kelton's eyes.

But a closer look made Kelton smile. "No big deal, man. You're bleeding a little, but it's just a scrape, hardly even a cut." From his pocket, Kelton produced the roll of bandage from his emergency kit. He worked quickly, noticing Hunter's extra wince, as he wrapped the bandage around that section of his leg. "That'll take care of the bleeding, no problem. But this next part . . ." Kelton picked up two of the fallen wooden ladder rungs. "I'm so sorry, buddy."

"Are you going to put a splint on it?" Swann asked.

"No, no, please, no," Hunter cried. "I can't take it."

"We have to stop the leg from flopping around if we're going to get you out of here."

Hunter nodded briefly, and Kelton went to work. He handed Hunter a smaller piece of wood, a split ladder rung. "Bite down on this." Hunter's growl was inhuman, from a place of unimaginable burning agony as Kelton straightened his broken leg. He was no doctor, but something definitely felt wrong, kind of lumpy, inside the leg. Flipping out his pocketknife, he cut the knot off one end of his hoodie sweatshirt's drawstring before pulling out the little rope. Next he took off his belt. It was cheap and a little worn, but it would do for this purpose. He had no time to think about it, but quickly placed two ladder rungs, one on each side of Hunter's knee, tightly against his jeans. Then he tied the two boards in place with his belt and hoodie drawstring. By the time he was done, Hunter's muffled howl had ceased and a deep silence fell on the chamber. Hunter had passed out from the pain.

CHAPTER 12

FOR THE SECOND TIME THAT DAY, THE PARKING LOT NEAR the racecourse off Warren Wagon Road was packed with snowmobiles. It had taken a while to assemble everyone involved in the search effort here, and Mike Irons hated having to do this, but he had no choice. In a moment he and Sheriff Hank Hamlin would make an announcement nobody would want to hear.

The rich actors caught up to him before he could reach the bed of the pickup from which he planned to talk to everyone.

"You are the one they call Iron Mike?" the woman said.

"Yes, ma'am."

"I'm Aurora Siddiq." She nodded at the worried-looking man next to her. "My husband Amir. Our daughter—"

"Yes, I know who you are," Mike said. What must these people be going through right now? Mike wanted to scream in frustration for not being able to find his nephew. He didn't have kids of his own. He couldn't imagine the anguish a parent must face to know her child was lost out there in the snow. It all made what he had to do much more difficult.

"I understand you've been heavily involved in the search for our daughter and the others," Aurora said. She looked around the snowy parking lot. "I know this is a bad night. That makes it even more important that we find the children quickly." Tears welled in her eyes. "We cannot give up. Amir and I would be willing to pay extra, considerably extra if it meant—"

"Mrs. Siddiq, I'm going to stop you right there," Mike said. Why did rich folks always think they could solve all their problems by throwing around their money like this? *They're desperate,* he reminded himself. *They'll do anything to get their daughter back.* Mike softened. He patted Amir on the shoulder. "Listen. This is McCall. We look out for our own. Swann's one of ours now. My nephew is also missing. We're doing everything we can to find those kids. I promise. But . . ." He tugged his beard. "Well, I have to make an announcement now, that you're not going to like, but the sheriff and I have agreed it's time. I'm sorry. Truly, I am."

With help from his friend Hank Hamlin, Mike climbed up in the bed of the pickup, slipping a little on the snowy surface. He took the bullhorn from the sheriff, switched it on, and addressed the crowd.

All right, folks. Quiet down, please. Listen up, everybody. I know none of you want to hear this right now. I sure as heck wish I didn't have to tell you, but we gotta face facts here. I know we still have three missing kids out there somewhere, and some of you, maybe all of you, are perfectly willing to comb the woods all night looking for them. That's one of the reasons I love McCall.

He looked out in the crowd and saw Hunter's father—Mike's

brother-in-law, David—and his other brother-in-law Rick, both looking about ready to throw up from worry. At least Yumi was safe, having a nice sleepover with her friend at the lodge. For once, she and Hunter hadn't been together. Mike wished Hunter was at the lodge too. He wished he didn't have to say this next part, which would be tough for everyone, and especially his own family, to hear.

But it's dark, and this snowstorm is only getting worse. We have no choice but to call off the search for the night.

There was some grumbling in the crowd, but Mike held up his hand and continued.

If we try to keep this up in a storm like this, we're going to lose more people out there. There's good odds that the three missing kids are together, and my nephew Hunter is reasonably skilled in the wilderness, so we hope wherever they are, they've found some shelter to hunker down for the night. The search will resume at first light. We'll coordinate everything from right here in this parking lot, so I hope to see you all back here right before sunup. The snow ought to have died down by then. Let's all go home, get whatever rest we can . . .

Mike swallowed hard.

And, you know, let's say some prayers. That's all I got. Good night.

He'd said, "Good night," but he knew it would be one of the worst nights possible, especially for the three missing kids.

"IS HE ALIVE?" SWANN WHISPERED DOWN TO KELTON. Hunter had finally stopped moving, stopped holding back his scream against the pain.

Kelton checked his breathing and nodded. He picked up the flashlight. "I'm going to throw this up to you. That way you can shine it down on me for better light while I have my hands free."

Swann laughed a little. "I'm not the best catcher. My old school didn't have much for sports."

"I'm terrible at sports too, but you must catch this," Kelton said. "If it falls and breaks . . . I don't know . . ."

He didn't have to say more. She'd been submerged in the nearly total darkness of the mine. Without the flashlight, none of them would ever get out alive. "You just make sure you don't throw it against the ceiling down there."

"Believe me," Kelton said, "that's just what I've been thinking."

Kelton moved closer to the hole. Swann leaned down over it, reaching out. He'd have to toss that thing about a dozen feet. He took a couple of practice swings, like a golfer before teeing off. "Here it comes."

He tossed it up in the air, the flashlight flipping end over end. Light, shadow, light, shadow, light. Dizzying. It was through the hole before her hands. It landed in her palms, but she bobbled it. It fell back toward the hole. Swann dove for it, collapsing to her belly at the edge of the pit and reaching out, catching the fatter lightbulb end of the flashlight in her fingertips. A flick of movement, and she had the thing firmly in hand. She finally let out a breath and whispered, "Sorry about that."

Kelton looked down at Hunter, then back up to the hole. "It must be over twelve feet. He can't climb. I can't climb and carry him." Kelton pointed to the rock wall at the close end of the lower chamber. "Shine the light over here." He ran his hands over the rock face. "Yeah. Can't climb this. Even if I could, the hole is back, like, two feet from the wall." He let out a breath and his hands clapped to his sides. "In the movies, these mines always have train tracks and little open cars. But no rails so far."

Swann watched him, feeling more and more hopeless, keeping the flashlight beam shined on him as he walked about. The flashlight bumped one of the wooden poles that used to be the side of the ladder.

Just as the flashlight hit the pole, the idea hit her. Was it possible? "Kelton, remember when we were partners in science?"

"What?" Kelton asked, sounding annoyed.

"Pulley. And ramp," she said. "Kelton, listen. "You were talking about rails. These poles could be our rails. And we . . . we . . . It will make it easier for us to pull him up, maybe keep him from moving around too much."

"We don't have a pulley," Kelton pointed out. "I only brought twelve feet of rope. It's not long enough for you to pull on and for me to tie to Hunter."

The light glinted off a worn snap on Hunter's discarded snowmobile suit. "Clothes! Kelton, we use Hunter's snowmobile suit. You can tie his to mine."

"Hmm," Kelton said. "Might be long enough."

"When the clothes rope is tied to the real rope and to Hunter, I pull, you lift and push, sliding him up the rails. Once he's up . . ." Then what?

"Once he's up, I'll tie the rope to me. You pull, I'll try to climb the rails. There are nubs of rungs in a few places." Kelton smiled.

Swann smiled back. It was the first tiny bit of hope they'd had. "All right," she said. "Let's do this."

A FEW MINUTES LATER, KELTON HAD FASHIONED A LOOP out of Hunter's snowmobile suit, tying it tight under Hunter's arms. He tied Swann's to that, twisting each garment like a rope. Both legs of each suit would be twisted together and stronger, same for the arms. It was hard to tie the outfits together like that, especially with his cold, slightly numb fingers, but he wanted this rope to be strong. To the clothes section, he tied the real rope, doubling the knots, making them tight. If this improvised rope tore apart, that was it. Swann would have to go for help, and that would only place her in terrible danger. Plus if the rope broke and Hunter fell again, this time onto his broken leg, who knew how bad it would be for him then? It might kill him.

"Are you ready for this, Higgins?" Kelton said, leaning over Hunter, who'd regained consciousness. It took a while, and it had caused Hunter a lot of pain, but Kelton helped him move to the two poles they hoped to use as rails. Hunter's face was red and sweat beaded on his forehead despite the deep chill in the mine.

With Hunter secure, Kelton tried to toss the other end, the real rope end, up to Swann. It took a few tries, but eventually

Swann caught it. She gripped it hard. Mom and Dad had always encouraged her to be a strong girl, but Swann figured they mostly meant she should be smart, confident, and willing to try new things. This was definitely a new thing, but she doubted very much that she had the physical strength to pull up a boy who weighed at least as much as, if not more than, she did.

Still, they'd rigged a sort of ramp, a rickety and very steep one, but it would help. And Kelton would be lifting.

"Hey," she said to the boys. "I'm going to tie my end around myself. Then I'll lift by backing away from the hole."

"That's a great idea," Kelton said. "Everybody ready?"

Swann wasn't ready. She'd never be ready for something like this. Who could be? Police or firemen, maybe. Strong people trained for rescue. No, she was not ready. More than anything, she wanted to be back home, under a blanket in her hanging chair up in her beautiful tower library. How had she ever complained about coming to Idaho? How had she ever complained about anything before? Everything had been great compared to this.

"Ready, I guess," Swann said.

"You can do this, Swann," Kelton's voice echoed from below. It sounded like he was talking to her from the other end of a pipe. "You're tough. I knew that from the first second I saw you. You say go, and we go, go, go. No stopping until Hunter's up there."

Did he really think she looked tough? No. That was just one of those sports pep talks guys seemed to like so much, stuff coaches said. *Just DO this, Swann! Stop worrying about stupid boy stuff.* "Ready. Set. Go!" Swann dug her feet in deep, slipping on the rocks, trying to find a good foothold, but finally she took a step back. Another step.

"I got you, Higgins," Kelton grunted. "Up you go."

The load lightened a little and Swann stepped back, back, back, the rope tied around her waist, her left hand pulling on the line ahead of her. She looked for a handhold. Something she could grab on to with her free hand to pull. Even with the flashlight placed upright on the floor, shining up to the ceiling to light everything above the hole, the room remained dark. The entrance to the chamber was still a solid five feet away. Hunter had to come up a lot higher than five feet.

"Got a foothold here, get ready for a big push," Kelton said. Hunter only groaned in pain.

The line relaxed, and Swann pulled ahead at least two feet. The rope was tight around her belly, making it hard to breathe. Her legs burned as she churned, forcing one step, then another. "Ple-ease," she groaned.

The rope gave a little more. She reached her free arm out, a foot or less from the chamber entrance. There was a big lip of rock there she could grab and pull. Tears welled in her eyes. She couldn't do this. But she had to do this. And it hurt so bad. Her whole body burned, muscles tight, pushing.

"Whoa!" Kelton shouted. "No, no! Hold on!"

The rope yanked at her gut and she slid on the rock. "Kelton!" She fell for a moment, sliding along the floor toward the hole, until she got back to her feet, counterbalanced by the rope.

"Got you!" Kelton said. "Sorry, man. I know that hurts." To Swann he called, "Sorry. I slipped there. Let's keep going."

Sweat beaded on her forehead and back. She bit her lip until she thought it would bleed. "I can't keep this up," she said through gritted teeth. She'd almost killed Hunter, nearly dropping him like that.

He doesn't think you're tough. He thinks you're a rich, spoiled SuperPop who's never worked and is helpless to do anything. Lots of people around town feel the same. Is that who you want to be? Forever your daddy's precious fragile princess?

"I . . . kill . . . the princess," Swann growled. Two steps. Her thighs flared with stabbing pain now.

Her fingers brushed the rocks at the edge of the chamber entrance, but slipped off. She groaned or gasped or cried and forced a big step. Then another.

"Got it," she hissed as she gripped the cold edge of the rock. Holding the rock allowed her to take some of the strain off her legs, to give them a little rest for a moment.

"I got a toehold in this hole on one of the poles," Kelton said in a strained voice. "Hang in there, Higgins, get my shoulder under you here to push up."

"Dude," Hunter choked out through the pain. "Did you just tell me to hang in there?"

Swann burst a short laugh and nearly slipped off the handhold. "Don't make me laugh, idiots!"

"I can almost reach the ceiling," Hunter said.

Swann dug in and step, pulled, stepped, along the wall outside the chamber. The wall was good. She could brace her feet and back against it like a brake, so she couldn't be pulled back.

"Can't help much anymore," Kelton said. "Hunter, can you reach—"

"Got it!" Hunter said. He made a sound like a mix of a baby's cry and a deflating balloon. "Hurtsobad. Got. Top of hole." More grunting, whimpering. "Can't pull. I can't."

"Come on, SuperPop!" Kelton called. "You have to help him. Pretend there's a grand opening at the mall. You just gotta get there."

Swann pulled the rope and stepped hard. "Hate you, Kel!" She wasn't stupid. She knew what he was trying to do. She was supposed to get all angry at him and show him how wrong he was by pulling Hunter up. Swann screamed. She stepped and clawed at the wall for new handholds to pull until her fingers bled. Tears and sweat ran down her cheeks. It would never end. Just the burn of lifting all this weight, and the pain of the rope and rocks cutting into her.

The rope jerked ahead. Swann took a few panicked steps forward, fearing she was slipping and Hunter falling.

"Stop! Swann, stop!" Hunter called.

"What?" she screeched.

"Stop! I'm up," Hunter said. "Oh, oh man. This hurts so bad. But I'm up."

Swann dropped to the cold rocky floor in the dark, and

sighed. She thought for a second that they should be cheering, celebrating this next-to-impossible rescue. But they were all fried.

"It will be easier to pull me up," Kelton's voice echoed through the mine like a ghost. "I promise."

She wanted to cry. Back in the chamber, Hunter lay on his back next to the hole, his eyes squeezed shut. There were tears on his face, but tears of pain. She wouldn't say he was crying.

So what if he did cry? Big deal. They were in a miserable situation. She wanted to cry too, even at the risk of fostering a fragile princess reputation. She ran her good hand over Hunter's damp forehead. "Are you all right?"

"I'm alive," he whispered.

"Not sure if I am," she said, freeing the rope from its loop around Hunter's chest. She tossed the free end down to Kelton, who looked back up at her with concern. "Are you OK?"

Swann shrugged. "Ready?"

"It will be easier this time, Swann. I promise. I figured out some climbing tricks, plus I have my arms and both my legs, and I'm not fighting against Hunter's pain." His expression changed. He had dropped all of the sports-style pep talks. He wasn't trying to trick her with the reverse psychology. "Hey, you know. I was kinda kidding about that rich spoiled stuff." It was hard to see, as it was so dark down there, but she swore his cheeks flared red. Maybe that was from the work of lifting Hunter. Maybe it was something else. "I said that 'cause I thought, you know, if you got mad . . ." He trailed off as Swann laughed. "What?" he asked.

"You really think you're that slick?" she asked him, still laughing. "Like I couldn't crack the code on your sneaky trick?"

"Oh." Kelton looked down, his face hidden in the dark. "Sorry. That was pretty stupid. I don't know what I'm doing, I guess. Just trying to help best I can. Your awesome plan worked. For Hunter, at least."

Swann stopped laughing. Oh, he thought she was making fun of him. He probably had a lot of experience with that, had come to expect it. "Kelton, I was just joking around with you. Not everything's an insult. I couldn't have pulled Hunter up here without you. Now, if you don't mind, I'm kind of cold and would like to get you up here so we can all go back by the fire."

The two of them exchanged another long look before Kelton nodded and tied the rope around his chest under his arms. Then Swann pulled and Kelton did his best to climb. The hard part was when he'd slip a little, and the rope would jerk her back. But Kelton had been right. It was much easier bringing him up to their level than it had been lifting Hunter.

When he was up, Swann put on her snowmobile suit, and then she and Kelton helped Hunter through the painful process of putting his on, keeping it as loose as possible around his injury by unzipping the bottom of the leg. Finally they all lay on the ground, filthy, aching, exhausted, and freezing.

"OK," Swann finally said. "That's problem number one million solved. What's next?"

CHAPTER 13

RETURNING TO THE ENTRY TUNNEL, KELTON AND SWANN worked to build the fire back up. Kelton had dragged the big ladder poles out there, so they'd have a lot more firewood. He doubted it would be quite enough, but they'd already had too much dangerous mine exploration and they'd have to make do with what they had. But even with a good fire going, the cold of the frostbitten night wouldn't let go of them.

"We have to close the tunnel entrance, or this fire won't do us any good," Kelton said. "Wind and snow coming in. I don't know what time it is."

Swann checked her phone. "It's nine thirty-two."

"A long time until daylight when we can try to get out of here," Kelton said.

Hunter lay shivering on his back, face scrunched up in pain, on the side of the fire away from the entrance, off to one edge of the tunnel to avoid the trickle of water from the floor ice the fire had melted.

"Snow wall?" Swann suggested.

Kelton smiled at her. "I was about to say the same thing." He looked at the snowy entrance and flexed his chilled stiff fingers in his gloves. "This is going to be a cold job."

"I'll help you," Swann said.

On a different night, it would have been easy to seal it off with a snow wall. But the bitter freeze didn't make for good snowman-ready packing snow. They could pile all the powder they wanted. It would never stand up as a wall. But by mixing the powder into a watery slush on the cave floor and using an upside-down snowmobile seat as a shovel, the two of them built a decent barrier.

The work dragged on, cold and cruel. The mine entrance wasn't very wide and a few times Kelton and Swann bumped together as they slopped on the slush. "Sorry," Kelton said as their shoulders touched while they packed in another section of the pre-ice mix.

Swann met his gaze and let out a shivering little giggle. "It's OK," she whispered. "It warms me up, a little."

What was he supposed to say to that? A Popular would know. They all spoke the same language, somehow gifted from birth to know the coolest things to say.

"Happy to help," he said. *You're an idiot, Kelton.* He changed the subject quickly. "We can't close the entrance all the way." He removed his freezing wet gloves to stretch his icy fingers by the fire. "Or we'll run out of air. Plus we gotta let the smoke out."

"Are you doing OK, Hunter?" Swann said.

Kelton looked away for a moment, trying to push away that weird feeling . . . what was it? . . . an imbalance, the awkward sense that he wasn't standing right or appearing the way he should, the idea of being out of place, in the way. What was the big deal if Swann talked to Hunter? The Pops stuck together with Pops. That's the way it was.

"Hurts so bad," Hunter whimpered. "So cold."

Swann looked to Kelton with worry. "Should we move him closer to the fire?"

"We move him much closer, he might end up burned." Kelton watched the guy. "I'm worried about him going into shock."

"I saw about that on a movie once, but I don't know what it is," Swann said. "I don't know what to do about it."

"I don't know either," Kelton confessed. "It was just part of the treat-a-casualty video I was talking about. Shock is bad, I guess. People can die from it."

Swann motioned to him like, *So what do we do?*

Kelton took a deep breath, trying to remember. "It seemed to me like a lot of the treatment things on the video were the same. We want the blood flowing through him good. So we loosen his clothing. And we gotta elevate his legs."

"No," Hunter moaned. "Don't move my—"

"Elevate his good leg." Kelton handed Swann his snowmobile seat, and she carefully propped his good leg up on it.

"So . . . what? We unzip his snowmobile suit?" Swann asked.

Kelton put some more wood on the fire. "Yeah. And we try

to get it warmer in here." He took off his own coat, once Swann had unzipped Hunter's suit, and draped it over the guy like a blanket.

"Kel, you're going to freeze," Swann said. "You've already had enough trouble with that."

Kelton kicked at a small stone on the floor, his cheeks a little hot after she used the nickname. "You and Hunter saved me. Now I have to help."

Swann looked at him a long time. Finally she patted the cold ground right beside her. "Come sit here," she said. "It'll be a little warmer if, you know, if we're not so far apart."

"Well, I . . ." Kelton began.

"Because of the wind," Swann said.

"Yeah, I was going to say the wind," Kelton said.

"Like in science class," Swann said.

Kelton nodded. "Yeah. Totally science. Because, like, the cold molecules." He nodded a lot. Did he usually nod this much? He forced himself to stop nodding.

"Yeah," Swann said. "If they, the molecules or whatever, can't get through . . ."

"It helps," Kelton said, slowly making his way across the cave and sitting down close to Swann. "There."

A long silence.

"Better?" Swann asked.

"Yeah." Kelton shrugged and his shoulder rubbed Swann's shoulder. "Sorry."

"I know I'm not about to starve to death," Hunter said. "But my stomach is seriously rumbling."

Kelton reached into his pathetic survival kit and pulled out the one bit of food he'd brought. "How about a late supper?" He shook the Snickers bar in his hand. He opened it, broke the nearly frozen thing more or less in half, handed one piece to Swann, and then leaned around behind her to hand the other to Hunter.

"But what are you going to eat?" Swann asked, her chunk of the candy bar almost to her mouth.

"I had a big breakfast," Kelton lied.

"No," Hunter said in his pained-voice. "This isn't right."

"Eat up," Kelton said. "You try to hand it back to me, I'll throw it on the ground. So just eat." They were quiet for a moment. The fire crackled. Then came the crunch of their biting off bits of the hard candy bar. "And you better like it," Kelton said. " 'Cause after that, all that's left is to draw lots to see which of us the other two will eat first."

"Ugh, don't make me laugh," Hunter complained. "Hurts too much."

After the Snickers, Kelton brought the other two clean snow to eat, so they wouldn't be so thirsty. They needed water far more than they required food.

"There's nothing to do now but sit here and wait for morning," Swann said, pulling out her phone. "Still no reception."

Kelton thought of teasing her about that. Of course there

was no cell phone coverage in the deep backcountry. In a mine. But he worried she'd think he was making fun of her. In a mean way. From what she'd said, the way she acted, he had the idea that she really did want to fit in here in this tiny Idaho town. He had to give her credit. SuperPop was trying.

Swann flipped through some photos on her phone, a few selfies with Morgan Vaughn and McKenzie Crenner, some photos in her mansion cabin. Some with her mom and dad. "I should save my phone's battery for its light, and hopefully to make a call the closer we get to town tomorrow. I guess I'm just so used to looking at it whenever I have to wait for something. It's like I don't even think about it. It's just there."

Kelton couldn't help but notice how long she had looked at the photos of her mom and dad. When she shut her phone off, he wondered if she thought that might be the last time she would see their faces.

They sat in silence for a long time, watching the fire. Eventually Hunter seemed to fall asleep, lying on his back on the rocky mine floor.

"Are you sure it's safe to let him sleep?" Swann whispered. "In a book I read once, they were super-worried about an injured man going to sleep."

"I think that's for concussions," Kelton replied. "I don't think he has one. After that fall, he's pretty lucky it was just his leg. Some of these mines have shafts that go hundreds of feet deep, or the bottoms are filled with freezing toxic water, or poisoned air that'll kill you." He shrugged. "I don't know. We have to let him sleep. He'll need his rest for the big day we have tomorrow."

Swann chuckled. "You sound like my mom."

Was she making fun of him? He knew he shouldn't trust her or any other Pop, but somehow he didn't think she was mocking him. "Last year, teachers were worried about me. Bad grades. Whatever. They made me talk to the school counselor."

"There's nothing wrong with talking to a therapist," Swann said. "My mother does."

"Sure," Kelton said. "I just meant that I was pretty down at the time about—" Popular or Grit, he didn't trust anyone close to enough to reveal all the crap he'd told the counselor. "About a lot of things. She mentioned one simple idea that a lot of people don't think about. She mentioned how much better people will feel about life and everything, after they've had enough sleep and if they're drinking enough water. I thought she was just another dumb teacher, but I figured, why not give it a try? Went to bed earlier a few nights. Drank more water. It really did help. Doesn't solve my problems, but it helps me deal better, I guess. Pretty stupid, I know."

"Not at all," Swann said. "How could it be stupid to want to feel better? At my old school, there was a lot of pressure to get perfect grades and be involved in many activities to try to get into a prestigious college."

"That's good, right?" Kelton said. "Get you a good rich life. Me? Teachers don't think I can do anything."

"You can do whatever you want," Swann said. "And it wasn't good. It was a nightmare. So much competition. I barely had any time for fun or for . . . life, you know?" She must have realized she was talking louder, because she checked to make sure Hunter was still out. "I started drinking all these energy drinks all the time, to help me stay up late to study, to get me through the school day." She looked at him. "It was miserable. Part of the reason my parents moved us out here. Mom introduced me to some more healthy tea and juices." She perked up. "You ever have kale juice?"

"What juice?"

"Kale," Swann said. "It's a superfood."

"Naw," Kelton admitted. "Nothing fancy like that."

"It takes some getting used to, but it made me feel so much more awake and alive. Wish I had one now. I'd share it with you."

Kelton didn't say anything. The photos and all Swann's talk about her parents just made Kelton feel worse and worse. What if they never made it out of this and she never saw her mom and dad again? Her parents would be crushed. They were probably already super-worried, and it was all his fault. His stupid shortcut.

"Or not, if you don't want any," Swann whispered lightly, leaning her shoulder into him. "But you should give it a whirl. You'd be surprised."

"It's not that," Kelton said. "I'm just sorry we're stuck here. This is all my fault."

Swann shrugged. "You told us to go back. You tried to warn us."

"If I hadn't dreamed up this failure of a shortcut, none of this would have happened," Kelton said.

"Maybe we should lay off the blame game," said Swann. "It seems like there's plenty to go around."

Kelton continued, "I'm so stupid. It's just, it seemed like an easy win, and the money I would have scored from selling your dad's sweet *Snowtastrophe III* snowmobile could have helped Mom with bills, so we wouldn't have to move yet again."

"You've moved recently too?" Swann asked.

Kelton looked down, fidgeting with a loose string at the bottom of his sweatshirt. "In about the last three years, we've moved maybe . . . ten times. And I'm tired of moving, especially since this duplex we're in now might not be very good, but it allows pets."

"And you have a . . . a cat or something?"

Kelton shook his head. "There's this dog. Don't know what his real name is, but he seems to like it when I call him Scruffy. Thing is, he belongs to this mean old man who lives in a crappy trailer. The man never pets that dog or nothing. Barely feeds him. When I pet Scruffy, I can feel all his ribs. That dog spends all his time chained up in this dirt patch in the freezing cold."

"That's terrible," Swann said. "I'm more used to these horrible little toy dogs that rich women carry around in handbags."

Kelton's chest beat heavy and he squeezed his hands into fists. "I take Scruffy my breakfast some mornings, or try to bring him some of my lunch after school. I was thinking, if that old man doesn't care about that dog, and I had all that money from selling that prize snowmobile, I could buy Scruffy. Take him home. Give him a bath and feed him right."

"That would be nice," Swann said quietly.

"Now I failed him!" Kelton said, a little too loudly. But what did he care if he woke up Hunter? No Popular would be quiet for him if he were trying to sleep. "Scruffy is going to spend the rest of his life freezing in the snow or mud with hardly nothing to eat. Nobody cares about him. Nobody! He could die, and nobody would notice. And why? What did he ever do wrong? What's so bad about him that he has to get crapped on and kicked around his whole life? And no hope and nothing to look forward to. Why's it gotta be this way?"

Kelton's eyes stung, and he turned away from Swann, waiting a moment before pretending to have to scratch his face so he could wipe them.

Swann patted his arm. "Hey, it's OK. You're OK."

Kelton pulled his arm away. "Sorry. I'm just . . . hungry and tired. Get all worked up about a stupid dog. It's just a dog. I don't care. For real."

He couldn't look at Swann, couldn't bear to see her mocking expression, or, worse, her look of pity. Pity the poor Grit.

She sighed. "Why do guys do that?"

"What?"

"Why do they try to act all tough like they don't care, when it's very clear you do care?" Swann paused for a long moment. "I know you think I'm a . . . a SuperPop or whatever, so you don't trust me. And that's OK. I can't force you to like me."

He risked a look at her right then, and the flickering firelight danced in her eyes and on her dark hair.

"But maybe, at least until we get ourselves out of this mess, you could maybe not lie to me?"

He wasn't sure what to say to that. Swann Siddiq was the most unusual Pop he'd ever met. He had no idea how to respond, except that if she wanted truth, he could add only, "It's getting late. We should probably try to sleep a little too."

Kelton put some more wood on the fire, and then sat there, head down, eyes closed, until he drifted off, dreaming of home.

CHAPTER 14

THE WORST THING ABOUT POWER OUTAGES WASN'T AS much the fact that there were no lights at night, but that all the lights sometimes snapped on in the super-early morning hours. And why did electric appliances need to beep when they reactivated? The noise and the light jolted Yumi from a great dream about—in her irritation she'd already forgotten.

Annette groaned. "What time is it?"

Yumi checked her phone. "Ugh. Six thirty-eight. Not even light out yet."

A bell rang. It echoed through the whole lodge and both girls screamed.

"What's that?" Annette shouted.

Yumi scrambled out of her sleeping bag and ran to where Grandpa's huge yellow plastic antique telephone rang on the wall. She lifted the enormous headset off the big claw thing and held it to her ear.

"That sound was a phone?" Annette hissed. "Thought it was a bomb or chain saw or—"

Yumi snapped her fingers for quiet, giggling. "Hello?"

"Yumi." It was her mother. "Is Hunter there?"

Yumi laughed a little. "No, Hunter is not here. Although maybe Annette wishes he—"

"Yumi, your cousin is missing. So are two other kids, Kelton Fielding and Swann Siddiq. Missing since last night."

Annette was about to object to Yumi's joke about Hunter, but Yumi frowned and shook her head.

Mom continued, "When was the last time you saw Hunter? Or any of the others."

"I haven't seen them since the start of the snowmobile race."

Mom explained how Dad and more and more people were launching a search in the woods surrounding the racecourse, and how the three of them had passed the first checkpoint, but not the second.

Yumi wanted to curse, but knew her mom would be mad. "It's all because of Kelton Fielding's stupid shortcut! I knew it. I told Higgins that following Kelton was a stupid idea. Swann must have gone with them."

"What are you saying?" Mom asked

"I don't know where they are, but I know which way they went. I'm, like, ninety-nine percent sure." Yumi explained it all to Mom twice. "I want to come help with the search."

"Absolutely not!" Mom was deadly serious. "You two stay at the lodge. You never know but maybe Hunter just got lost and is on his way back there now. You need to be there when he arrives."

Yumi rolled her eyes. "He's not on his way back here. He's somewhere up Storm Mountain on the old gold mine road. Just . . . fine. Uncle Mike knows the trails better than anyone. Have him call here, OK?"

After an overlong exchange of "I love you" and "Be safe," Mom finally hung up.

Uncle Mike called a few minutes later. "Remember Stone Cold Gap?" Yumi told him. "And that old gold mine road over the pass? That was Kelton Fielding's shortcut. Hunter was real mad about it, planning to follow and beat Kelton at his own cheat. I'm sure of it. Think about it. The turnoff for that jump is after the first checkpoint and before the second. They got stuck trying to get over the mountain."

"You're sure?" Uncle Mike said.

"Check a map if you don't believe me."

"Yumi," said Uncle Mike, "you may have just helped save their lives. I gotta go."

The line went dead, and Yumi hung up the huge headset on the big hook. She looked at her worried friend. "Annette. We need to start packing soup, blankets, hand warmers. I think there's a tiny propane camp stove somewhere. There's a snowmobile out in the garage and it will be light soon. We are going to find Higgins and the others."

THAT COLD NIGHT HAD OFFERED A ROUGH, UNEVEN sleep, the kind of rest where you're really not sure if you've slept at all, but instead spent most of the night thinking about how much you wish you were sleeping, drifting into strange thoughts, thinking maybe you finally really were sleeping. Sitting up all night, head drooping down, cold hard rock beneath her, Swann hurt pretty much all over by the time she noticed the view over the top of their snow wall beginning to brighten.

She must have slept a little, because the fire had burned down to embers and the cold had swept back in. She could see her breath in puffs before her. There was a little wood left, but she didn't dare move to put it on, for fear of waking Kelton, who seemed to be sleeping, leaning against her, and because she didn't want to leave her cold place for something colder.

After a few minutes, Kelton finally stirred, licked his lips, and opened his eyes. He looked at her, took a deep breath, and smiled. Then he glanced around the mine and his happiness fell.

"I was hoping it was all a dream," Kelton whispered.

"You were hoping I was in your dream?" she teased.

"What?" Kelton whispered. "No. I mean, well, yeah. I'd rather be dreaming about you than stuck in this freezing mine."

"What do you think?" she said quietly. "Is it light enough to move out?"

Kelton winced as he turned his head slowly toward the mine entrance, hand on the back of his neck. "Yeah," he grunted. "But let's warm up first."

Kelton slid over to the remaining wood supply and carefully

worked the embers until the fire burned again. Gradually, the chamber began to warm a little.

Kelton returned to her side, but didn't sit as close as he had last night. He nodded toward Hunter and whispered, "Look at him, sleeping away. All cozy under my coat."

Swann snorted. She was glad to see the guy was OK. "As cozy as someone can be with a busted leg."

They were not comfortable for long. Hunter woke up shortly after Kelton began breaking down the snow wall at the mine entrance. The packed wet snow had frozen pretty hard. He had to chip away at it with a wood shard. Finally, he'd cleared a narrow door on one side of the mouth of the cave. Outside, the world had transformed, everything, including their snowmobiles, buried under at least two feet of snow, and all of it shining blazing white in the early morning sun.

"Good weather for our escape from all this," Kelton said, squinting his eyes as Swann joined him outside.

"But how do we get Hunter out?" Swann asked. "I don't think he can drive his own snowmobile.

Kelton looked at her. "I have an idea about that. It's not a good one, but nothing about this is good. First, we gotta dig out our sleds. You're right. There's no way Hunter is driving himself back home. We should have just enough gas, at least enough to get back to walking distance to find help."

It took a long time, but Swann and Kelton finally dug out the three machines. Hunter kept apologizing for being unable to help.

"Come on, man," Kelton finally said after what seemed like Hunter's millionth regret about his not digging. "We've said it's fine. If I was hurt like you, I hope you wouldn't be expecting me to kill myself trying to help dig. You're driving us nuts. Just try to relax."

Swann looked at him for a long moment after he said that. Was she agreeing with him, grateful he'd spoken up? Or did she think he was being too harsh to a guy with a busted leg?

At last, the sleds were cleared, and Kelton had a chance to look over Hunter's and Kelton's, popping off the engine covers to make sure the workings inside weren't jammed with snow.

Swann came to watch his work. "You really know what you're doing with all that?"

A Pop impressed he could get his hands dirty and work with machines. Kelton shrugged. "I've been learning all I can about my sled for a while now. It looks complicated, but once you take the time to figure out the different parts and what they do, it's kind of simple, really. Only it's hard finding money for parts." A problem someone like Swann would never have.

Kelton locked the covers back on both sleds. He held his hand up to shield his eyes from the sun to look at her. "Your phone still have a charge?"

"Not much," she said. "I'll put it in your plastic emergency bag."

"And that inside your snowmobile suit," Kelton said.

They packed snow over the remains of their fire and then

parked the rented snowmobile inside the mine. "Thanks for getting us this far." Swann patted the machine.

After a few pulls, they started Hunter's snowmobile, then Kelton's. Then came the hard part. "This is gonna hurt, Hunter," said Kelton, "but I can't figure another way to get you out."

"Going to hurt?" Hunter grunted in pain. Then he fought hard to keep from screaming as Swann and Kelton carried him out of the mine.

"Keep moving," Kelton said. "Let's just get the worst of the pain out of the way all in one go."

They did not have anything for Hunter to lie down on, so they tried the next best thing. Swann helped tie Hunter back-to-back with Kelton, using Kelton's emergency rope.

"I'll try to lean forward so you can lay back and keep your body and leg straight," Kelton offered. "It'll be awkward driving, and I can't promise no bumps. But I'll do my best. Swann, you want to follow and watch, make sure he's OK?" Kelton pointed up the slope. "Getting around will be hard, but we know we basically gotta go that way, follow the pass in that direction, up over the top, down the other side. Eventually we'll reach the creek at Stone Cold Gap, and after that, the trail. Then we'll find help, no problem."

"Easy!" Swann shouted.

Kelton and Hunter chuckled, but Kelton could feel Hunter shaking, feel his many little groans of pain. Of course, Swann had been joking about this being easy. Kelton knew very well that this was going to be the worst day of Hunter's life.

Kelton driving his own sled, and Swann following on Hunter's, the three of them set off on the long journey home. Kelton took it slowly, carefully scouting ahead for what looked like the smoothest way forward. But this was backcountry sledding through thick powder. It could never be a smooth ride. Kelton tried to use his upper body as a shock absorber system, doing all he could to reduce the impact of each bump.

It was mostly useless. Hunter groaned. He sort of hissed in pain. He whimpered. Several times he screamed. Kelton promised himself that whatever else happened, he would never in his life tell anyone about hearing Hunter cry.

Doing his best to keep his eyes on the trail, Kelton turned his head to call back to Hunter. "Hang in there, man. We're coming up over the top of the ridge. Be heading back down real soon. I'll get you out of this. I promise."

Hunter only moaned. The guy didn't even sound human anymore.

Kelton's sled ran well, ripping through the newly fallen powder, steering smoothly around trees and rocks, pushing forward. For all the difficulty, he couldn't help but love the feeling of power he controlled in this machine he'd fixed up and made to run. "Come on," he said quietly to it. "We're counting on you to bring us home. Just keep on going. Nice and steady, now." Kelton blipped the throttle to get it up over a rise, and although the road was long, and they had a tricky basin to navigate, he was thrilled to see the downslope before them. The long way out.

With apologies to Hunter, he turned to look back and make sure Swann still followed them. She offered a quick wave, right with them. SuperPop could drive that sled.

The snow ahead was a collection of big puffs with some dark undersides. Could be rocky terrain. There was enough snow to make almost any area passable, but Kelton had to think about Hunter. He eased the sled around it, watching a big drop-off twenty yards farther to the left and picking up a little speed on a gentle downhill slope on the smoother path. This would work. They'd make it back.

EVEN THOUGH HUNTER'S FACE WAS HIDDEN BY HIS HELMET and he was bundled up in his snowmobile suit, the tension in his body was obvious. Following a few yards behind, Swann watched as he suddenly squeezed himself extra-hard about the shoulders or threw his head back, and a moment later she felt the bump that had knocked his leg around and sent that fresh stab of pain through him.

She followed Kelton around some rough-looking territory. "Geez, cut it close to the cliff, Kelton," she said to herself. Nobody would hear her through the helmets and over the motor roar.

They were up over the top now and heading downward. She

smiled. They were finally going home. Once home, she would spend hours safe and warm in her library. Maybe put on an audiobook. Something she'd listened to before, because she'd probably fall asleep.

The front end of her sled flew up, her engine whined louder. She was slipping backward.

To her left, the snow crumbled and fell away. Nothing beneath it! She screamed. This didn't make sense. The front of her sled rose higher. She was sliding backward. A giant crack in the ground, to her left, and the snow falling down it, like sand through a sieve to her right. Her sled was sliding back into the crevice, big enough to swallow her and her machine.

Swann panicked and maxed-out her throttle. "Please! Go! Go!"

So much loose powder before her, all spilling down her snowmobile's track into the pit behind her. She was losing ground. She couldn't pull out of this. A thousand terrified thoughts flew through her mind in an instant. *I'll die Never see Mom and Dad again Never grow up This is going to hurt so bad.*

KELTON FELT THE HARD ELBOW IN HIS RIBS, HEARD Hunter shouting. Afterward, he wasn't sure if he could tell anyone exactly what had happened. He saw Swann, sled skis way up, backsliding into that crevice. And he moved without thinking. Braking hard, he untied himself from Hunter, Hunter untied himself, or they worked together. Then Kelton threw himself off his sled, rolling over the top of the snow to avoid the slow high step through the deep. When he was close enough, he stomped down into the powder and reached for Swann's arm. "Grab on to me! Come on!"

SWANN FELT A HARD SLAP ON HER ARM.

Kelton had appeared out of nowhere, his grip an iron claw digging into her forearm, and her shoulder ached as he yanked her toward him. She ran, jumped, pulled on Kelton. His other arm slapped around her shoulders and pulled. Behind her, the sled's engine whined higher. A thud. Crunch. Scrape. Finally a loud crash.

She hit the ground hard, landing on top of Kelton. When something like this had happened in *Snowtastrophe III,* the hero character looked into the beautiful eyes of the girl he had just rescued for a romantic moment before the two of them kissed.

There was no romance now. Landing on top of Kelton had hurt. And he groaned. Swann was pretty sure her knee had accidentally hit him where a guy hurts the most. There was no eye stuff because they both wore helmets. And helmets or not, there would be no kissing.

She climbed off him, moving up the minor slope away from the surprise gap in the ground. Idaho could be like that, a mountainous jigsaw puzzle of rocks, cliffs, slopes, and crevices. The snow hid a lot of it, and had almost taken her down.

Kelton groaned again as he slowly crawled through the snow

after her, away from the crevice, smoke rising from the fire of the wrecked snowmobile below.

When they'd finally reached Hunter by Kelton's sled, Swann removed her helmet. "I'm so sorry, Kel."

Kelton took off his helmet. "Oh." He spoke through pain. "I think . . . it'll pass . . . someday. You probably would have been worse . . . if you had fallen."

"What do we do now?" Hunter said quietly after a long quiet. "Three of us and one snowmobile. We can't all ride one sled back. Especially not with my leg."

Swann flopped over on her back, head resting on the freezing snow. A new shiver went through her. They were trapped again.

CHAPTER 15

YUMI CURSED. AGAIN. IT WAS THE THIRD TIME SHE AND Annette had managed to get her snowmobile stuck out here. She remembered her uncle Mike saying if you didn't get stuck, you weren't snowmobiling hard enough. Well, she wasn't interested in sledding hard. All she cared about was finding her cousin and the other two.

Finally, they'd rocked the snowmobile and blipped its throttle, easing it ahead inch by inch until its track bit, and they were going again. In the past, Yumi hadn't been interested in backcountry snowmobiling, but now she openly hated it. How could anyone think this was fun? She tried to push out of her mind the dark thoughts of all the horrible things that might have happened to Hunter and the others. The two of them had hurried to pack and head out even before they had light. Then they'd had to power through slushy mush in that shallow point in the creek to avoid the jump at Stone Cold Gap. She knew exactly where they had to go, but this was still all horrible. She and Annette rode out after them, crowded onto the snowmobile with both their fronts and backs laden by backpacks stuffed with supplies to help their friends. If there was still time.

Yumi drove that snowmobile up Storm Mountain farther and farther, hoping she was anywhere near where Kelton had led them. Stupid shortcuts.

"Yumi, look!" Annette shouted close to Yumi's helmet as her arm shot forward, pointing up the hill. Before them, a definite column of black smoke rose into the sky. "Do you think it's them?"

"A fire burning out here in all this snow?" Yumi shouted back. "Someone must have started it. Let's go find out. Get that radio ready!"

Yumi cranked the throttle and sped up. Driving this wasn't easy, but that column of smoke was like a magnet. More than that. Yumi had read about black holes, super-gravity events in space that sucked in stars, chunks of planets, even light itself. That was the kind of pull this smoke, this dark beacon possibly pointing the way to her cousin and best friend Hunter, had on her.

"Come on you"—Yumi cursed—"thing. Go!" She cranked the throttle, desperate to go faster and faster, up the hard slope.

"Do you think it's Hunter?" Annette shouted to be heard through their helmets and over the engine buzz. "Like he started a fire to help people find him?"

"Don't know!" Yumi yelled back. "Hope so! Just taking forever to get there to find out." She didn't want to tip the scales of fate by even mentioning what would happen if the fire went out and the smoke vanished.

"WE CAN'T JUST SIT HERE," SWANN SAID. "IF NOBODY comes along, we sit out in the open and freeze? No way."

Kelton sat sideways on the snowmobile seat, leaning over, head in his hands. "We can't fit all three of us on one sled, especially not with Hunter hurt like he is. You want us to leave somebody behind? Leave someone to die, maybe? Or else somebody walks out of here alone, maybe back to the mine for the other sled, leaves the other two? But that could be just as bad for the walker. End up lost, then frozen, then . . ."

"So we're just out of options?" Swann asked. "I don't care. I'll take the risk and walk out of here if I have to."

"Swann, I can't let you go. You know—"

"You can't stop me either."

"Will you two please shut up?" Hunter said. "You make my leg hurt even worse! Nobody is . . ."

He trailed off and they all perked up, hearing it at the same time, a faint buzzing, almost like a distant chain saw. Swann exchanged an excited look with Kelton. This wasn't a saw. She'd become all too familiar with the sound yesterday and today. She'd heard it all over McCall through the winter.

"A snowmobile?" she asked.

Kelton sprang to his feet and looked around, as if trying to find the direction from which the noise was coming, but with all the echoes, it was difficult to figure out, sometimes, the origin of a sound.

At the top of the ridge, she couldn't tell how far, came a flash of red and black, hard to see through a haze of blowing snow. But in the next instant it was clear. "It's a snowmobile!" She jumped up and down, waving her arms over her head. Kelton did the same. "Hey! Over here! Help! Please help!" The sled stopped, little more than a dot in the distance.

"No," Kelton said, desperation in his voice. "No, they have to see us. Please."

All three of them yelled, Hunter lying in the snow, Swann and Kelton standing on top of Kelton's snowmobile waving, hoping so much they'd be seen.

"YUMI, LOOK!" ANNETTE SCREAMED. "DOWN THERE! TWO of them, by that snowmobile."

Yumi had seen them, of course. That's why she'd stopped for a moment, to get a careful look and make sure it was real. Because what she thought she saw was only the greatest sight of her whole life. Her cousin could be down there.

"But why only one snowmobile? Where's that fire coming from?" Yumi asked. "And I can only see two people? Do you see three people? Oh no. Did they lose someone?"

"Only two," Annette said. "Let's get down there!"

"Wait!" Yumi said. She pulled from her pocket the best handheld Motorola radio she could find at the lodge and checked to make sure it was on channel 9, the emergency traffic channel everyone was using on the search. She keyed the transmit button. "Emergency! Anyone on this channel. Please respond. This is Yumi Higgins. I think I have eyes on at least some of the missing snowmobile racers from the McCall Winter Carnival snowmobile race. I'm . . . I'm up on the old gold mine road between Big and Little McCall mountains. Ahead of us is a snowmobile and at least two people. There's a fire coming from somewhere, smoke coming up. Can anyone hear me? This is Yumi Higgins. I think maybe I've found the missing racers." Her voice tightened up as she finished. "I hope I've found them." She let go of the transmit button so she could receive. "Come on, someone pick that up. Tell me I'm not totally out of range of—"

Yumi, this is your uncle Mike, the voice came on the radio, a little scratchy. *I know about where you are. You sure it's them? Over.*

Yumi radioed back, "I'm not sure. I can see two people in the distance. One snowmobile. Something's burning, maybe down over a cliff." Had someone gone over the edge? Did the fire mark the worst? "I don't know who it is, but I wanted to try to call for help while I'm at the top of the ridge. I'm about to head down to see if I can help. Um. Over."

When you get to them, stay there! I'm on my way with help. Keep trying to call. Let them know they're going to be OK. Over.

"Will do. This is Yumi Higgins, signing off. Um. For now." To Annette, she added, "Let's go see if that's them."

"HE SEES US!" SWANN SHOUTED. "HE'S COMING THIS WAY! He sees us!" She threw her arms around Kelton and squeezed. He nearly fell off the sled seat they were both standing on, but somehow managed to regain his balance to hug her back, if the one-armed squeeze could be called a hug. More just kind of an excitement thing than a hug. Grits and Pops didn't hug. Not really. Grits and SuperPops? Impossible. For real.

Finally, she let go and jumped away, down off the sled and instantly down past her knees in the snow. Kelton watched the sled coming down the hill closer and closer. "I think there's two people."

"Seriously?" Swann asked.

"Hope they have an aspirin or something," Hunter said.

"Hold on, Hunter," Kelton said. "I think we're finally going to get out of this."

An eternal few minutes later, the snowmobile slid to a stop next to them. The driver pulled off his helmet. But he was a she. And she was Yumi Higgins. She took one look at Hunter, lying on the snow next to Kelton's sled, and gasped, running to him. Annette removed her helmet too. "You guys OK?"

"Oh yeah," Kelton said. "We've had an awesome time."

"Hunter's leg is broken," Swann said. "He's in a lot of pain."

Yumi looked up from Hunter's side, tears in her eyes. "What happened?"

"No big deal, cousin," Hunter said. "Fell down a hole in the old gold mine."

"You were in a mine?" Yumi shouted.

"We needed the shelter to warm up," Swann said. "Kelton was pretty cold after we pulled him out from under that avalanche."

"That second avalanche," Hunter added.

Yumi hugged her cousin. "Higgins, you idiot." She paused, bit her lip. "I'm so glad you're alive. If you'd gone off and died, I would have killed you."

Annette Willard, proud reporter for the school newspaper and website, watched it all, openmouthed. "Oh, this story is going to make such a good article." She chuckled. "But first, we have candy bars, cans of soup, blankets, hand warmers, a thermos of hot cocoa, bandages, flashlights, dry clothes. All we could carry." She joined Yumi at Hunter's side, giving the guy a hug.

"You're going to be OK, Higgins," Yumi said. "Uncle Mike is coming. He'll bring others." She looked up at Kelton and Swann. "You're all going to be OK."

Kelton let out a long, relieved sigh. "Well, they might take a while. Meantime, I'm hungry." He rummaged through one of the three backpacks the girls had brought. A little mini camp stove. A can of soup. Double Noodle! A can of baked beans.

"Or what do you think, Hunter? Swann? Should we wait until we get back to eat?"

"Start cooking!" Swann said.

Hunter laughed and coughed, offering a thumbs-up.

Kelton started working on their feast right away, using his sled's seat as their table. Swann stepped up, a huge smile on her face. She held out her gloved fist, and he bumped it, because in that moment, when they'd finally reconnected to the outside world, he couldn't make himself care so much about the different worlds from which the two of them had come.

CHAPTER 16

A FEW WEEKS AGO, WHEN MOM AND STEVE WERE OUT late, Kelton had found a DVD of this old movie called *Die Hard* on Steve's movie shelf. Mom would never have let him watch it if she knew. It was awesome-violent, but with a lot of adult stuff. At the end of the movie, after the terrorists were all defeated and the hostages rescued, the movie's action hero guy and his wife were hanging around with a bunch of cops, police cars and ambulance lights flashing, safe again. That was the scene back at the snowmobile race starting line.

Except his mom almost screaming his name as she ran and threw her arms around him didn't make Kelton feel like much of an action hero, and of course Kelton didn't have a wife. "You're OK, baby," Mom whimpered, hugging him to her a little too hard. Normally, that kind of thing would be super-embarrassing in front of everybody, but he hadn't been hugged like that in a long time, and it was a nice change of pace to be warm.

This big guy, Mike Irons, or Iron Mike as the other rescuers called him, Hunter and Yumi's uncle who had been the first to find them out there after Yumi and Annette—he stood with Hunter's mom and dad as Hunter was loaded on a stretcher. "You did good, Hunter," Iron Mike said. "You really held in there. Doctors will fix you right up." Hunter offered a weak smile.

Kelton broke free from his mom's embrace and jogged to Hunter's side. "Hey, man. I hope you're better soon. And, you know, thanks for digging me out from under that avalanche."

Hunter smiled. "Thanks for splinting my leg and helping to get me up out of that chamber."

Kelton didn't know what to say to that. He only shrugged.

"Maybe we could get together sometime," Hunter said. "Like we used to do? When my leg's better, we could try some ice fishing or something."

The Populars all played everything cool, like they didn't care about anything, but Kelton couldn't hide his smile. "Yeah. I don't want to think about more ice right now, but I'm sure later, after I've had a chance to warm up, that would be great. Maybe catch a sweet trout."

Kelton backed away as the paramedics lifted the stretcher up into the ambulance.

"We'll be right behind you, Higgins," Yumi called to him. She looked up at her father, a guy who had been, like, a real action hero in the war in Afghanistan, and who now had his arm around her shoulders. "Right, Dad? We're going to the hospital too?" He nodded.

Annette held up her phone. "My parents texted it's OK if

I go as well, as long as I'm home early enough to get ready for school tomorrow."

The ambulance squawked its siren for a second to warn people to clear out of the way as it rolled toward the road. Yumi and her family headed toward their cars.

"Hey, Yumi," Kelton called as they passed. "Annette. Thanks for finding us. For the soup and blankets and stuff."

Yumi stopped and looked at him with that intense glare Populars had that made a Grit feel so stupid for whatever dumb thing he'd said or done. She approached in three swift, determined steps, and threw her arms around him, squeezing him close. "My cousin says you splinted his leg, lifted him out of that mine, and treated him for shock."

"Swann and I worked together to get him out of that lower chamber," Kelton admitted.

Yumi backed up, her hands on his shoulders at arms' length. Was she about to cry? "He might not have made it without you. I won't forget this, Kelton."

Annette watched it all, taking notes. "Yeah, great job." She nodded at Swann. "Maybe we can talk more later? For the school paper? People will want to read about how you all made it through."

When they were gone, Kelton said quietly to his mom, "Everyone's acting like it's so great, but this was a disaster. All my fault. Me and my stupid shortcut."

"Shh." She patted his back. "For now, we're all just so thrilled to have you back safe."

"Mom, there's something else I have to tell you. I needed a part for my snowmobile. Plus the entry fee. Well, I had this plan to win the race and have plenty of money to pay back, but—"

"Steve's stupid knife?" Mom asked. "I hate that thing. What'd you do, pawn it?" She laughed. "Serves him right."

"But it was kind of stealing," Kelton said. He must have suffered brain damage in that avalanche, to be turning himself in like this, but after everything that had happened he couldn't resist coming clean.

Mom only sighed. "We'll figure out a punishment later, if you insist on beating yourself up over it, but I think the greater crime was me dating that loser in the first place." She squeezed him in a one-arm side hug. "Now, what do you say we go home, get you something to eat, and watch some good movies? You need to rest."

Nothing had sounded so good in a long time.

SWANN FELT LIKE SHE WAS IN THE MIDDLE OF A SIDDIQ sandwich, and she loved every moment of it. Mom on one side, Dad on the other. Cynthia a few paces away, watching with a smile. A Siddiq sandwich with a side of Cynthia.

Margo approached, tapping away at her phone like always. "I think this whole thing will trend very well," she said. "If I move quickly, make some calls to some contacts, I bet I could swing an interview on the *Today* show. And of course all the entertainment sites are just warming up the buzz."

Dad sighed. "Margo, thanks. You're the absolute best publicist, but right now we're just happy our girl is safe. Could we get some space, please?"

Margo pressed the phone over her heart. She smiled as she then tapped away on the phone again. " 'Just happy our girl is safe,' " she said as she walked away. "Perfect tagline."

Swann noticed Kelton, a few meters away, watching. He shot a questioning glance at Margo. Swann rolled her eyes, agreeing with him. She was crazy.

"Oh, my little Swannhilda," Dad said. "We were so worried we'd lost you. I couldn't . . . I can't handle . . . I'm nothing without you. Please don't do anything like that again."

She knew he was trying to express love, relief that she was OK. But it only brought on a fresh wave of guilt. "I'm sorry," she said quietly. "It was stupid. I know. I thought if I could win the race . . . well, you'd be at the finish line to award the prize, and you and I . . ." She shrugged.

"You did this trying to impress me?" Dad said.

"Impress both of us?" Mom asked.

"I guess," Swann said. "I'm sorry."

They both hugged her again. "Swannhilda," Mom said. "We're the ones who are sorry. We brought you out here, away from your school and all your friends. And then we've been so busy."

"We're moving back to California," Dad said. "This is obviously not working here."

"No!" Swann said, sure for the first time of this much, at least. "I want to stay. I like it here. Besides, moving back won't change anything."

They were all quiet for a moment. Dad finally spoke up. "You're right. But things . . . things here are going to change. Mom and I are going to be around more. I promise. We'll go boating and hiking and fishing and everything. Together."

"I'd like that," Swann said. "Very much."

A WEEK LATER, KELTON SAT ON THE SOFA AT HOME, rereading Annette Willard's article for the school paper, "Three McCall Students Survive Dangerous Ordeal." An ordeal? Was that what it had been? It had certainly been the talk of the school all week. Teachers had welcomed the three of them back almost as if they actually wanted them, even Kelton, in the school. Even the Populars were asking about what had happened, to the point where he was growing tired of talking about it. He was just glad some old guy from out of town had won the race and taken the big prize, so he didn't have to listen to Bryden Simmons or someone brag about his awesome new snowmobile.

Mom was at the kitchen table, sighing and fidgeting with her hair as she tried to figure out the bills. She opened another envelope and unfolded the contents, reading for a moment before she gasped and her hand slapped the table. "What?" she mumbled. "No. Is this . . . Can't be." She traced lines on the letter with her finger, reading carefully. "Kel!" she said. "This is . . . I mean, I gotta check on this, to see if it's legit, but this says our landlord sold our house."

"I'll start packing." Kelton sank down on the sofa. "Again."

"No!" Mom stood up. "This says the house is now owned by some . . . New Frontiers Real Estate. Listen to this, whatever this means. 'Senior New Frontiers management has reconsidered property asset valuation as it correlates to market invoice index margins and determined the evaluation relative to monthly lease values.'" She looked at him. "I never went to college, but does any of that sound like it means anything?" She tapped the letter. "But this part is clear. It's saying we owe two hundred and fifty dollars less in rent every month."

Kelton sat up.

Mom spun around, holding up the letter. "Two-fifty a month? Kel, I could catch up on bills! I could take a few less shifts at work. We could go hiking together. This is . . . I gotta call the number here. Make sure this is real, but Kel. This could change everything!"

"We won't have to move?" Kelton asked hopefully.

"We won't have to move for years!" Mom threw the letter up in the air, tears in her eyes. She looked at him with a big smile. "We're going to be OK, Kelton. I think we're going to be just fine."

The doorbell rang. Kelton went to answer it, and almost took a step back in surprise. Swann stood on the doorstep, wearing her dark fancy jeans and a puffy purple coat.

"Hey," Kelton said. Like an idiot.

"Hi," Swann said brightly. "Are you doing OK?"

"Of course," Kelton said. He jerked his head back toward Mom. "In fact, there's this whole thing with the rent, and—you know what? Never mind."

Swann smiled warmly and nodded.

Kelton's cheeks flared red. "Oh my gosh. Do you want to come in? It's cold out here, and—"

"No, that's OK," she said. "Thank you. I can't stay long." She pointed to the big yellow Jeep parked in the street. "Mom's waiting in the car."

Kelton was relieved she didn't want to come in. He couldn't imagine what a mansion-living SuperPop like Swann would think of their crappy little place. "Oh," was all he could think to say.

"I got some flowers for Hunter," she said.

"Yeah," Kelton said. Kelton had wanted to get flowers for Mom once, for her birthday. He couldn't believe how much they cost. He'd ended up getting her a Snickers bar instead.

Swann shrugged. "Actually, Margo, my parents' publicist, had them sent over to his house. She won't stop going on about the media reaction to our . . ."

"Our disaster?" Kelton filled in for her.

Swann laughed a little. "Yeah." She was looking at him, and somehow Kelton didn't know what he should say. He wasn't even sure how he should stand. What was wrong with him?

"But I didn't want to just have Margo or someone send you a thank-you," Swann said. "I wanted to tell you in person, without everybody else all around. Thanks for everything out there. You kind of saved me."

Kelton wanted to kick himself. Why were his cheeks so hot? "Well, I didn't dig myself out from under that avalanche or get that life-saving fire going. So thank you."

She smiled, and wow, was this girl beautiful. For real.

"Oh!" she said. "I almost forgot. Hang on. Stay right here."

Before Kelton could say anything, she ran back to the Jeep and opened the back door. There was a little yip, and in the next instant a gray furball shot out the door and splashed down in the snow. It bounced up, snow on his fuzzy face, silly pink tongue hanging out the side of his mouth. He barked and ran toward Kelton.

"Scruffy!" Kelton shouted, and walked out on the snowy front steps. Who cared if his socks got all wet and cold? "Scruffy!" The dog jumped into his arms, and Kelton lifted the thirty-pound pooch right up. "Scruffy, what are you doing here?"

Swann had rejoined them. "You were right about the old man in that trailer. What a jerk. But it turns out that, well, after some negotiating, the dog was for sale after all. Only my mom doesn't want a dog in the house, messing up her decorating and everything. So maybe you want him?"

Kelton bit his lip, hard, trying to get control of himself, and he buried his face in the dog's stinky fur, trying to wipe his eyes. This was the kindest thing anyone had done for him in his whole life. This SuperPop was really pretty great.

"Thank you," he finally said, when he was sure he could get the words out clearly.

"No problem," Swann said. "Thank you for taking him. I guess I should have checked with my parents before buying a dog."

The two of them—with Scruffy, the three of them—stood close together on the cold and cracked front sidewalk, sun shining brightly on the snow all about them.

"Well," Swann said. "I better get going. Mom's—"

"Just one question," Kelton blurted out. Swann raised an eyebrow. "Swannhilda?"

Swann's cheeks reddened. "It's from an old opera." She stepped very close to him. "And that . . ."—her lips brushed his ear as she whispered—"is a secret." She remained there for a long, bright moment. "See you around, Kel." She kissed his cheek.

Then she backed away, smiled at him, and hurried off to the Jeep, leaving Kelton standing there, stunned, unaware of the cold, holding on to Scruffy.

Kelton looked down the block to where that yellow Jeep,

with Swann riding inside, waited for a moment at a stop sign. He smiled, not sure what his future held, but for the first time in a very long time, he was eager to find out. "Scruffy," he said. "Did that just happen? Did you see that? Was that real?" The dog stretched out his neck and licked Kelton's face. "Ugh. Scruffy!" He laughed, giving the dog a loving squeeze. "Now you ruined it."

ACKNOWLEDGMENTS

AT THE END OF THIS SECOND BOOK IN THE MCCALL Mountain series, I am absolutely loving the time I've spent with these characters in this fictionalized version of the small Idaho town of McCall. I had a lot of fun writing this book, and for that privilege, special thanks go:

To the wonderful people of McCall, Idaho, whose incredible community is such terrific inspiration for this series. Dear reader, if you haven't had a chance to visit McCall, you're really missing something special. McCall is the best.

To Rebecca Van Slyke for her friendship and the inspiration of her courage and strength.

To Rollo Van Slyke for critical guidance about snowmobiles. Any snowmobile-related errors remaining in the book are entirely my fault. Also, thanks for fixing the ice maker.

To the great team at Norton Young Readers for all their help with both *Hunter's Choice* and *Racing Storm Mountain*, with special thanks to my incredible editor, Simon Boughton, for all his patience and insights as we worked out how to get Kelton, Swann, and Hunter into a whole lot of trouble and back again.

To my greatest friend and ally in the writing world, my agent, Ammi-Joan Paquette, for connecting me with Mr. Boughton and Norton Young Readers. Thanks for your patience with me, for putting up with each brilliant-novel-idea-of-the-week, and for all your help.

To my daughter, Verity, for being so patient while I worked on this book, and for her encouragement while she listened to me read this book aloud during the month she was enrolled in Dad Kindergarten during Covid lockdowns.

And to my wonderful wife, Amanda, for unlimited support and encouragement, in writing and in life, these last two decades. Amanda, you are my life.